THOWARD'S QUARTERLY FICTION #55

Edited by
Howard Watts

Cover Artist

Howard Watts

Contributors

Anthony Thomson
Antonella Coriander
Douglas J. Ogurek
Howard Phillips
Jacob Edwards
Len Saculla
Mark Lewis
Rafe McGregor
Stephen Theaker

Contents

Editorial

9   Drunk and in Charge of a Magazine
Howard Watts

Fiction

17   The Departure
Mark Lewis

23   Our Sad Triangle
Len Saculla

29   The Little Shop That Sold My Heart
Howard Phillips

35   This Alien I
Antonella Coriander

55   The Stone Gods of Superspace
Howard Phillips

97   My Place
Anthony Thomson

The Quarterly Review

*Reviews by Stephen Theaker, Douglas J. Ogurek,
Jacob Edwards, Howard Watts & Rafe McGregor*

Audio

164   Life, the Universe and Everything, by Douglas
Adams (MacMillan Audio)
Jacob Edwards

Books

169 Jacaranda, by Cherie Priest (Subterranean Press)
Stephen Theaker

171 Lone Wolf 21: Voyage of the Moonstone Collector's
Edition, by Joe Dever (Mantikore Verlag)
Rafe McGregor

177 Patchwerk, by David Tallerman (Tor.com)
Stephen Theaker

179 The Sign in the Moonlight and Other Stories, by
David Tallerman (Digital Horror Fiction)
Rafe McGregor

Comics

183 Brightest Day, Vol. 1, by Geoff Johns, Peter Tomasi
and chums (DC Comics)
Stephen Theaker

185 Days Missing, by Phil Hester, Frazer Irving and
chums (Archaia)
Stephen Theaker

187 Ex Machina Book One, by Brian K. Vaughan and
Tony Harris (Vertigo)
Stephen Theaker

189 Goldtiger: The Poseidon Complex, by Guy Adams
and Jimmy Broxton (Rebellion)
Stephen Theaker

190 Predator vs Judge Dredd vs Aliens: Incubus and
Other Stories, by John Wagner, Andy Diggle,
Henry Flint, Alcatena and chums (Rebellion/Dark
Horse Books)
Stephen Theaker

192 Y: The Last Man, Vol. 4: Safeword, by Brian K.
Vaughan, Pia Guerra, Goran Parlov, and José
Marzań, Jr (Vertigo)
Stephen Theaker

194   Zenith: Phase Two, by Grant Morrison and Steve
       Yeowell (Rebellion)
       Stephen Theaker

       Films

196   10 Cloverfield Lane, by Josh Campbell, Matthew
       Stuecken and Damien Chazelle (Paramount
       Pictures et al.)
       Douglas J. Ogurek

200   The Boy, by Stacey Menear (Huayi Brothers
       Pictures et al.)
       Douglas J. Ogurek

202   Deadpool, by Rhett Reese and Paul Wernick (Fox)
       Douglas J. Ogurek

206   Gods of Egypt, by Matt Sazama and Burk Sharpless
       (Pyramania et al.)
       Douglas J. Ogurek

209   The Witch, by Robert Eggers (Parts and Labor
       et al.)
       Douglas J. Ogurek

       Games

213   Fallout 4 (PS4) by Bethesda Softworks (Bethesda)
       Howard Watts

       Television

217   Ash vs Evil Dead, by Ivan Raimi and chums
       (Starz/Virgin Media)
       Stephen Theaker

218   Fear the Walking Dead, Season 1, by Robert
       Kirkman and chums (AMC)
       Stephen Theaker

221   Jessica Jones, Season 1, by Melissa Rosenberg and
       chums (Marvel/Netflix)
       Stephen Theaker

223   Sherlock: The Abominable Bride, by Mark Gatiss
       and Steven Moffat (2entertain Ltd)
       Rafe McGregor

       Notes

228   Also Received, But Not Yet Reviewed
       Notes by Stephen Theaker

229   About TQF

Drunk and in Charge of a Magazine

Howard Watts

Okay, I borrowed for Bradbury – but why not? If you're going to borrow from someone, borrow from one of the best.

It's been a bit of a dilemma putting this all together. So many options ran around my mad head, options for formatting and art direction, and all before I considered the content. Alex Bardy's work for the BSFA publications he expertly lays out pointed me in various creative directions, but then I realised I was running away with someone else's style while looking after someone else's baby (or rather young adult, by magazine age standards) abducting them for a month or so with the possibility I'd spoil them with too many sweets, cream cakes and letting them stay up late to watch inappropriate Saturday night TV – which is kinda all of it – but that's another story...

I realised all too late that all the silly ideas I had would only serve to betray what TQF is all about. Saying this, I set to work, trawling through stories and editing. Oh what a job! I do not envy Mr Theaker at all – it's not an easy task, and not one to be dismissed as simplistic or something to simply jump into for the hell of it. To be honest, I tried to push it to the back of my mind as I sat in the local, but the job kept resurfacing to the forefront of my thoughts, and with it, the many and varied insane options. The more ale I consumed, the more these ideas (like little daemons, perched upon my slumped shoulders) shouted for attention. I kept this all to myself, refusing to share both my enthusiasm and trepidation to those that know me as an "arty type bloke" – only mentioning the job to a fellow writer I've known for twenty odd years – a guy of mad imagination and shirts, creator of bizarre circumstances in his writing. He looked up from his pint and grinned across the table to me – and that's when it struck me. "I'll give you a month," I said loudly, grinning back, "write something for me." He obliged of course, and I thank him greatly for his dedication to the work, (as I do to all the writers in this issue) amid the hectic life he leads with a new wife and sick mother to both cater for. The story came and I sent it straight back. "Not weird enough," I said. "You're holding back." It was then I knew I was really getting into this "guest editor" role.

So, what I have for you here, dear dedicated Theakarian is hopefully an enjoyable read, and that's all that (for me) really matters.

The Media

It's been an interesting few months, leading out of the winter and into the spring / summer. Saying that and looking out of my lounge window over to Seaford Head while typing this, it's sleeting! Sleeting near the end of April. Madness!

I admit I was excited by the return of the *X-Files* mini-series. Oh the heady days of the 90s, watching Scully looking the other way as something unworldly showed itself to Mulder and us the viewers. Pure SF pantomime 'twas the *X-Files* back then. Pity this new series fell far short in every respect compared to the original season's tales. Just grab every popular conspiracy theory, wrap 'em all up together and there's ya plot. Nah. Didn't work – and that fact was sadly displayed by the performances. I wanted to believe too, but honestly couldn't bring myself to.

One door closes as *The Walking Dead*'s latest season concluded, with a very nasty reveal in store for us next season, while another door opens with the return last week of *Game of Thrones*, which will undoubtedly contain many nasty reveals, and hopefully a few nice ones during this new (non book adaptation) season. I can't say enough good things about these two shows – both refuse to pull any punches when it comes to the "reality" stakes – and by this I don't just mean the graphic violence both manage to carry off perfectly, I mean the quality of writing. Relationships and all their varied emotional twists and heart-breaking turns are illustrated superbly by these two shows. So no, *The Walking Dead* is not just about zombies, and *Game of Thrones* is not just about boobs and dragons. Both shows are about people, our human condition, and these people are perfectly illustrated as they cope with circumstances none of us will ever experience during our lives, and some inevitable real world circumstances we hope we never have to.

Flash and *Arrow* continue to entertain me – good clean and sometimes silly fun. "There's a bank job at so and so!" Then "Team Arrow" manage to arrive at the scene of the crime just as it's taking place – usually at night. How the hell they manage to suit up with all that leather / spandex, masks, boots and weapons and arrive just in time and adopt the best tactical positions is great madness, but, true to comic panels the show emulates, I guess. *Flash* holds my interest more with its parallel reality storyline. Genre TV simply lacks a damn good SF set in space series. There was that bounty hunter thing on SyFy, but it just looked too plastic and tough as old boot leather – the acting and storylines sadly enjoying identical descriptions respectively. Please, where's the next *Babylon 5* gonna come from?

There's a new mag in town. I regularly read *SFX*, *Sci-Fi Now*, *Locus*, *Empire*, *Total Film* and *Starburst*, mostly. Then I stumbled upon *Geeky Monkey*. Now, I am in no way associated with the mag, nor anyone that works on it – I just believe it's a breath of fresh air for the inner geek / nerd in me, and perhaps, you. While the first two mags mentioned above will cram their pages with genre info (sometimes with identical storylines / interviews / cover photographs, depending what's flavour of the month), to the point where the reader has to reach for a magnifying glass to soak up all the content, *Geeky Monkey* will focus with great depth upon a particular genre staple or three per issue. Then, you'll turn the page to read about a long forgotten piece of gaming hardware or software title, or a roundup of the latest gadgets. It's big and brash – lots of detail but at the same time space amid its large format pages – worth a look next time you're in Smiths. It's a real luxury mag with a refreshing style.

Convention Season Is Almost Upon Us

It's been a couple of years since I attended a fan gathering. Brighton Film and Comic Con, scheduled for the first weekend in June, sparked my interest – I'm not good with any kind of lengthy travel for medical reasons, so the temptation of a con, "just down the road" to my birth town sparked my interest. Unfortunately at the time of writing, there's only *ONE* comic guest, a few from film – the rest, *Doctor Who* actors. Now, I've nothing against *Who* at all – I grew up with it and still watch it, but if you're going to run a con, at least assemble a guest list which *resembles* said con's theme. I don't want to go along to see Mr Whateverhisnameis, the guy that played Stormtrooper #73 (he's third from the back in scene 5 of the deleted scenes in *Star Wars TFA*). My point is, why is it so easy for other cons to assemble a cracking guest list? It seems, leafing through the latest issues of *SFX* and *Sci-Fi Now*, that if you travel to London and head north, the more chance you have of attending a con with a varied line up of top notch guests. That's a shame for a city that was once the town that hosted the 45th World Sci-Fi convention, back in 1987. My first con, a con where I found myself in a lift around 11 a.m. with Brian Aldiss and Harry Harrison, arguing in well-mannered good spirits about the talk they were about to give. I believe it was Harry who had a pint of ale in his hand. At the same con I also very briefly met Gerry Anderson, Forry Ackerman, Jim Burns and Ray Harryhausen. I sometimes wonder whom I walked past that I didn't know of at that time, at that con? Perhaps something will spark my interest that's not too far away during the season.

My Reading

Prague Art and History, by Tim Porter. I'm going to attempt a horror story, and wanted to set it in Prague during the late 17, early 1800s. Being impatient and not able to find much on the city via a Google search, I decided to cop out and set the story in London. I then wandered into a charity shop the following week (Seaford's full of them) and found this book – 75p. It's a great book with old maps and lush photographs, so I can steer my characters around the city and describe their surroundings in detail. There's nothing else on the bedside cabinet, I'm ashamed to say. At the moment, I'd rather write than read during my spare time – so I have the above story to get to grips with, plus a time travel thing that's finished and needs a damn good slap with a damp editing keyboard, and an Unsplatterpunk story for Doug's guest editor edition of TQF, which I haven't started, but its entirety is all in my head. Once these are out of the way, I must continue with the follow-up to my first novel.

That's really all I have to say, other than I hope you enjoy this issue. Many thanks again to the contributors and a big thank you to Stephen for trusting me to babysit his young adult, and giving it a final polish of Theakery love on my behalf.

Cheers!
Howard.

P.S. Remember that "Write a short story to this piece of art" competition we set back in issue 52?

If you don't, see the page opposite to be reminded of the art, and then read the winning story straight after! The runner-up story follows that. (And then there are three stories from our regulars that arrived too late for the competition.)

The Departure

Mark Lewis

Nima watched the skies empty, how had it come to this? Her mind had been made up, she had promised herself she would leave with the others. Join the new start, with her bondsman, Bron. Yet here she stood with her mother and brother, among the dejected ones who would stay to the end and die with the planet. The end was estimated to be only days away, when the sun would finally go out.

The great and the good (or the privileged and paying) had gone, a shell government, mainly Opposition politicians and out-of-favour elder ministers remained and no-one listened to them.

Nima's mother said empty soothing words, which barely even registered. Worse, she caught a wry smile on her brother's face. He tried to hide it, to play the supportive close brood member but Nima knew him better than that, saw the cruelty behind the smirk. She knew his mind, that he was left behind, so he would have a grim satisfaction in her remaining too. She had chosen to stay behind with him, to look after their mother for this short time rather than take her freedoms and new hope with Bron and start a new brood. Her mother was calcifying. It was a genetic trait on Nima's mother's side of the family. It had crept up on her gradually over the years, so slowly, but surely. Each year her skin would be slightly harder and thicker, she would be slightly less able to move until one day her body would set, her eyelids and mouth would seal over; she would become unable to move. This could happen long before her mind ceased to function, and she would live, a statue, kept alive in the family home by tubes drilled through the granite that would be covering her own body. This is how Nima remembered her grandmother, her incarceration in her own body had lasted for years until her mind followed suit and solidified into brain death. Although Nima was relatively young and supple, it had already started, with a marked difficulty in moving her fingers.

At least her mother, and ultimately Nima herself would be spared her grandmother's fate, as the sun would give out long before even Nima's mother would find her body fully calcified. As it was, she was at the stage where she needed assistance to walk and to perform more complex manual tasks. This was why Nima's mother had given her own place up, to a young scientist. Nima's brother had been furious, he had neither the status or the independent funds to bribe his way off planet. He had complained, in confidence to Nima, that it seemed that only those able to threaten or bribe their way on were able to get tickets. Or, he added, but it was a sore point, use family connections. He had explained that he did not understand why mother had given her ticket to someone outside her own brood; a respected scientist but also someone who had been perceived as a disliked rival.

He had resigned himself to playing the dutiful son and remaining behind to care for his mother, with her condition. He was fortunate, in that his skin followed his father's line with the softer skin that would never calcify, even though he was more likely to contract diseases. Evolution gave and evolution took away.

Nima had accompanied Bron all the way to the launch fields, all the way into the passenger tube. She had stopped while he walked through the airlock, then backed away when he was safely through and the door sealed. The hurt in his eyes had spoken volumes; the life they could have had together, the new life they could have grown, now would never be. He had tried to leave, but it was too late, Nima having stalled until the last moment. She knew him too well, he would have stayed with her, even with death being inevitable, the romantic idiot, so she had given him no choice. Bron managed to override the sealed locks; his genius for electronics had earned both their places on the ship; no, it had been more than that. He had been unable to make eye contact when she had asked him just how he had been able to get them both into the departure fleet. He was protecting her from something, now it was her turn to protect him. The door swept open, he started to come out.

"No," she had said, extending a hand and repelling him back. Like her brother, Bron was soft-skinned and could not match her for physical strength.

"You have to come," he said, "the warp would kill you." It hadn't been tested on hard skin, as it hadn't been anticipated anyone would be so close, but Nima would take the chance of her skin holding out. She roughly handled Bron back in, sealed the door again, ignoring his protests, and this time it was too late, two ship hands caught him and held him back, as the door locked again.

Nima was buffeted as the reality warp that powered the ships started up. As short as she knew her life now to be, she still prayed, to the great brood mother, in heaven, deep underground, that her hard skin would protect her from its effects. A kin with soft skin would have been killed by the effects of the warp, Nima felt her pale stone skin start to flake off, flying upwards, then settling to the ground like spent ashes. As the ships took off, and went into the distance, she would forever be marked, her skin cracked and mottled.

The warp settled down, leaving Nima on her knees, her hard skin battered and flaked and her heart broken. She went to join her brood mother and kin brother, who had stood at a safe distance behind mundane barriers that protected all from the effects of reality warp.

Later, when their mother had gone to bed, Nima quizzed her brother. How had he taken all this so lightly? His golden light glowed through his soft skin, the way it did when he was happy. Her brother told her what was so funny. At last, he told her what her mother had told him.

The announcement had not yet been made, but it would be soon. This was not an abandonment by the great and good, it was an exile. A revolution, a way of exiling the corrupt and the bad. The large numbers of undesirable elements had fled the planet and their reality warp drives would preclude them from overhearing any communications from their planet. It had been true, the only way to qualify for the trip had been through corruption, bribery or bullying.

"Even the Overfather?" Nima had asked.

Her brother laughed and said, "you're so cute, Nima. Of course he was corrupt. How do you think he got to be Overfather?"

"That makes sense as far as it goes. But mother would have let me board the ship. To be with them? The corrupt elite, the bullies, the gangsters."

"She knew you loved Bron, for all his faults, that's the nice version."

"The not nice version?"

"She wanted to spare you from watching her calcify. Spare herself from seeing you follow her."

"You should have told me."

"Loyalty to my dear old brood mama. I'm not a good kin but I wouldn't break maternal confidence."

"So those of us left behind, what for us? A utopia,

we'll be governed by the honest remnants of the council?"

"I told you you're cute."

"What of Bron? I could have saved him if I'd known. I knew mother didn't like him, but to let him go out there, to the great void..."

"Remember the lengths everyone had to go to for a place on a warp ship? He inherited his ticket from a specialist who died of a nasty accident. Bron was not the soul-kin you thought."

"So some of the worst scum have left us, what have we gained?"

"We're going to live. That has to be good enough. And try for something better."

"It's not just me who's cute," Nima said. "The most corrupt certainly, but we'll be run by those who thought up this cruel plan, and the councillors and everyone running the world who just weren't as effective at being corrupt as those we've got rid of."

The next time Nima saw her mother, even though the great announcement had been made, she did not speak of the departure, or Bron, or the conversation with her brother, and they never would. Nima saw already that her mother's mouth had begun to grow over, starting at the side, it was only a matter of time before she would not be able to talk.

Yes, Nima would live, perhaps a long life. The planet's death sentence had been a lie, the short life expectancy of those unable or unwilling to lie, bully or bribe their way on to a ship had been fiction. But so too, she was now free to watch her mother calcify, and then in turn, to slowly feel her own skin and joints harden, barely noticeably but surely, year on year, until she too was trapped in her own body, free to go insane, locked in, until her mind too solidified. With the apocalypse a non-starter, Nima was sentenced to a normal life.

Mark Lewis *has recently had work published in The Four Seasons anthology from Kind of a Hurricane Press, and in collaboration with fellow Clockhouse London Writers in The Masks anthology by Black Shuck Press. He has also had fiction and poetry widely published in the independent press, including the British Fantasy Society Journal, Escape Velocity, Scheherazade, Estronomicon, The Nail, and others. He has also written and performed in pantomimes. More of Mark's writing can be found at: http://syntheticscribe.wordpress.com.*

Our Sad Triangle

Len Saculla

I have been here on Altabran Three for so long now that I don't notice the noxious gases any more. The filters in my outer shell-form cope admirably with all regular forms of atmospheric pollution.

Carey likes to joke, "If you gave us a whiff of pure oxygen now we'd all be high as kites."

David and I smile even though we've heard the quip a dozen times. David once muttered to me, "I don't recall the reference; what on earth are kites?"

"Something from Earth," I answered, making a mental note to perform a follow-up comp check but somehow always neglecting to do so.

On the rare moonless evenings, the night sky is wonderfully speckled here. The thin air reveals a glittering array of unfamiliar constellations – including Sol if you know where to look. They are luminous beacons that mark the starry limits of our prison. Like convicts of old – yes, I have researched that part of Terran history – we labour in the daytime, putting in the hours, constructing, preparing the ground for the settlers who will come eventually. Buildings, domed parks, hydroponic farms, leisure centres... The Matter Enforcer bends to our whims, a triumph of science mated with alchemy, turning base elements into any compound structure or material we require.

I have researched much of Earth history and culture. David and Carey call me "Harry the Historian" when they are in a good mood. It's important to know where you came from. Even if you don't actively remember it these days.

"Pioneers with a magic box," Carey once called us. She is the true philosopher of our crew.

Returning to our home ship, we are greeted by the hanging cadavers of our preserved fleshy originals. Why do we keep them? Is it some sort of sentimental wish that we can one day go back to these weak, virtually immobile and useless carcasses that we once knew as our own skins? Only the transfer of our brains and subsequent consciousnesses to the shell-forms has kept our existence here viable.

"Routine time," Carey announces.

"Who made you captain?" David responds.

Ignoring their regular spat, I take on nutrients. I no longer miss the days of eggs on toast for breakfast, spaghetti bolognese or pizza, Coca-Cola and coffee, ice cream and cake. The pre-flight training that all of us were required to undergo knocked those urges out of me pretty quickly.

Refreshed, I perform a few more checks. Deterioration of our original form continues at a minuscule but definite pace. Less than a hundredth of a percentage point every day... but the days have been many. One day soon we will have to let our Earth bodies die and accept that we have transferred over permanently to our artificial humanoid shells... which themselves are less than perfect.

Altabran Three has two moons and tracking and considering their progress has been one of the consistent joys of our time here. Of course, machines can do all the calibrating and recording but lunar objects have held a fascination for people since we first evolved. No algorithm or series of coding can truly reveal the emotional ties and psychological effect that they evoke in us. I was much younger and more naturally curious when we first arrived here and I would spend much of the evening gazing upon these irregular yet fascinating objects, feeling their curious pull like I might have done near the roiling sea back home. This link with lunacy is one of the things keeping me sane, keeping me human for all that my true body has badly decayed and my shell replacement is doing likewise.

"Hark at the poet," David used to comment when I more regularly kept nocturnal watch on the orbiting satellites. Now he spends most evenings sullen or complaining. Or arguing with Carey. Our sad triangle seems to always be on the point of fracture.

Carey has lately fashioned herself a mirror which hangs on the edge of her designated section of the communal quarters.

"My shell skin's starting to peel again," she moans. "I'm flaking away like paper in a sandstorm."

"Fix it with the Matter Enforcer tomorrow," David answers.

"I'm not sure I will. I don't want to be some pampered, plastic bimbo. A couple of imperfections will give me character. What do you two think? Am I gorgeous?"

"Best-looking woman who ever lived on Altabran Three," I tell her.

"Thanks – for not much, Harold."

I haven't bothered reminding her that her adopted flesh is already essentially a plastic derivative. This is not a time and place for naturally beautiful women.

"You'll do until someone better turns up," David quips and I am glad that he has taken the heat out of the situation.

Tasks over, we can settle for some proper rest. I set the dream machine to offer images of calmness and let myself go into shallow sleep.

But I don't stay in the happy valley for long. Their voices are tense, full of clipped tones and poorly suppressed anger. They argue like an old married couple. I suppose if these emotions have to come out then I should just be glad that I am mostly left out of the firing line.

Then their tone changes, becoming conspiratorial.

"We can't go on holding this secret from Harold," Carey whispers. It's not fair to him."

"It's not been fair on us, either. I'm getting fed up maintaining this charade for his benefit. How long before we admit that he's fully grown up and can handle the harsh truth?"

"Shush, David, you'll wake the little mite."

"Little mite? He's taller than either of us. We can't keep mollycoddling him. He's been an adult for years now, whatever we think. He needs to know the full truth."

"We'll tell him tomorrow. Before work detail. Which he may decide afterwards is totally pointless."

Their voices fade. I appreciate their undying love for me, the strong tie that binds them together even though individually they might have decided to go exploring further, alone, or else might have packed it all in as a lost cause. I shall feign surprise when they offer the full reveal tomorrow... if they do. I shall be the good son and pretend that I don't already know the awful truth: that there is no second expedition or rescue mission on its way from Earth; that Earth has problems of its own that are on the brink of being solved catastrophically; that we three are here on our own for the duration.

Parents, eh? They never realise quite how much their offspring knows.

Time to sleep. And dream of the two moons of Altabran Three.

Len Saculla *had a story entitled "Zom-Boyz Have All the Luck" in Theaker's Quarterly Fiction #52. He has also had work published in the BFS Journal, Wordland, Unspoken Water and anthologies from Kind of a Hurricane Press in America. In 2015, he was nominated for a Pushcart Prize.*

The Little Shop That Sold My Heart

Howard Phillips

Pierre's wife had done everything she could to help him achieve his dream, which as it turned out was to run a shop called *Green Ties and Jam*. It sold nothing but green bowties and green jam. That may sound limiting, but let your imagination range free across fields of verdant flora! Gooseberries, grapes and kiwi fruits were just the beginning. Spinach, cabbage, peas, cucumber, lettuce: if it was green, Pierre had it turned into a jam and sold in his shop.

"Is it very successful?" I asked, the first time he took me there, mid-morning on a cold day in March.

He shrugged as he unlocked the door. "How can anyone judge success? It is what it is. My dream was to open a shop that sells green bowties and green jam. I have done that." He opened the door with a flourish. "Whether anyone chose to buy anything from the shop was irrelevant to my dream."

"But it would be nice," said Mrs Samuel, or Britti, as she liked to be called. She was a little taller than Pierre, with shoes that slapped the floor when she walked. "It's difficult to keep it going without any customers."

I smiled at her in what I hoped was a sufficiently patronising way. "It's hard to understand how we poets think. Isn't it, Pierre?"

"Poets, yes." He kissed Britti on the forehead and thanked her for driving us to the shop. "I shall see you this evening, dear heart."

She frowned at me and left. I do not think she was at all convinced of the threat to her husband's life, or of the need for my presence. She would be easy to remove from the picture, I told myself, before immediately regretting it. This was the pendulum that swung through my days. In the centre, happiness at having found Pierre and being able to keep him safe, to the right where I planned to steal him from his wife, to the left where I hated myself for such perfidy, and back to the centre where I was just happy that he was alive.

"I don't think she likes me much," I said to Pierre.

"Why would she?" he replied. He paced the shop, making sure everything was lined up and front-faced. "She sees the way you look at me."

I held my breath till he spoke again.

"But don't worry, I haven't." He looked me up and down and laughed, dismissively.

It hurt my feelings, I must admit. Though no longer at my most youthful, my looks not enhanced by my years of alcoholism, I was still considered by some to be worth the trouble of a second glance over the shoulder.

"Oh, stop it, Howard," he said. "I'm a married man, and I could never betray the trust of my wife. Unless you asked very nicely."

I decided to act as if the conversation was not happening, and made my usual circuit of the shop, searching for traps, listening devices, cameras — any sign of foul play. As usual, there was nothing, though the peculiar label on a jar of broccoli preserve made me stare hard: three ancient statues against a background of rushing stars. For a moment I lost myself in it, but then my attention returned to Pierre. I felt very tired, all of a sudden.

"It's very good of you to do all that for me every day," he said. "Keeping me safe from harm. Guarding my body. Saving my skin. But don't you have a job to go to? You've been here for weeks."

It had been a month. I was staying in a bed and breakfast that charged me an exorbitant rate to have the newspaper delivered. The couple who ran it were entirely charming, and delighted to have a room taken in March, though I could tell they were curious about the source of my income.

"I am independently wealthy," I told him, while crouching to check under the till.

"Oh!"

He fell silent for a minute or two, as we both went about our daily routine. He seemed pensive. I went over to look him in the face.

"Did you want to ask about it? I don't want to have any secrets from you."

His demeanour had somewhat changed. I could tell I had gone up in his estimation, in a way that had not at all happened when I showed him a poem of mine. I didn't let it bother me. Any interest was better than none.

"I suppose so," he said. "I am reliant on your protection, after all. What if you are a terrible fellow of some sort? A ruffian, a scoundrel, a gangster?"

"I have been called a scoundrel and a ruffian before, and much worse in the press. Do you not remember the Great London Bacchanal, for example?" He looked at me blankly. "Well, never mind, that is nothing to do with my money. It comes from various sources. The adventure on the Ghastly Mountain. *The Fear Man*, the album I recorded with The Sound of Howard Phillips. Everything I did with Howard Phillips and the Saturation Point. None of this rings a bell?"

He shook his beautiful head blankly.

"Well, it all made me a tidy sum, and though I often spent it unwisely I don't need much to live, and what remains, plus my royalties, is more than enough to keep me comfortable."

"The goal of every poet," he sneered, turning away.

I talked to his back. "The poetry doesn't make me any money. Nor do my novels."

He turned to look at me with laughter in his eyes. "You write novels? You?"

"I have written a few, based on my adventures."

"Oh, memoirs. Almost as bad. But they don't sell?"

"I am sure they sell in reasonable quantities," I replied, trying not to be provoked by his insouciant derision. Beautiful and carelessly cruel. How could I be anything but entranced? He was a cat and my heart was the mouse. "But I earn nothing from them, after losing all rights in perpetuity to my fiction to Stephen Theaker."

"Lost them? How?"

"A late night game of *Scrabble*. Or *Bloodbowl*. Or *Illuminatus!* He never gives the same answer twice. It doesn't bother me. He publishes them with the minimum possible amount of amendment, not caring if they will be commercially successful or not. If an author's goal is to sell a million copies they should avoid his publishing house like the plague. If their goal is to keep their artistic integrity none could be better, even if his lack of tampering has as much to do with laziness as principle."

"Sorry, I stopped listening," said Pierre. "Could you be a dear and get a new box of oakleaf jam from the cellar? It doesn't look like anyone is going to kill me today."

He began to throw out-of-date jars into a black bin bag. I tamped down my upset and went to do as he had asked. I had never asked him how he made his money. I suspected the shop was losing a great deal of it, and was supported only by Britti, who worked twelve hours a day as an accountant. I think I too would have worked twelve hours a day if he wanted me to. The foolishness of love!

As I reached to flick on the switch for the cellar light I felt the slightest movement of air against the exposed skin on my wrist. Instinct took over. Not natural instinct, but the instinct ingrained in me during my training in Ban Village, at the base of Mount Ban-Mossow, where I had met my friend the Mountain Drummer.

I cancelled my plans to turn on the light and dropped to the ground, rolling three times to the left and then three times to the right. I didn't hit anything, but a grunt of frustration came from the darkness.

My target!

I curled into a semi-circle and performed what in Ban Village they called the *flipping crescent*, twisting my body to fly across the ground at my supposed enemy. Even in the bright daylight of a Himalayan village this move is extremely difficult to counter, since your body is at first below, and then above. In darkness even more so!

I collided with the creeper in the dark, and knocked them off their feet. My hip let me know that it had come into contact with a metal object of some kind, but was unable to say as yet what it was. It didn't feel as if I had been wounded. That could have been shock.

Never mind, no time to check. I stretched out my body like a bow and let my arms and legs swing against my enemy with incredible force, the move known as *archer's folly*. All four limbs connected, eliciting a distinctly feminine "uff". I took no chances, performing the same move three times until I was sure of the lurker's unconsciousness.

I got to my feet and picked up her gun, for that is

what it was, then turned on the light. It was the Indian woman from the base I had destroyed in January, all five feet of her!

"So you escaped," I said, upon seeing her eyelids flutter. By then I had tied her hands and feet together and leant her against a crate of mushy peas jam. "Perhaps it was a mistake to leave that door open."

"A mistake that shows you have a conscience," she said, blowing cobwebs from her face. "How can you work with this monster? Protect him? Do you know the things he has done?"

"I don't have any idea what you mean," I said, and I genuinely didn't, not then. "Why don't you tell me?"

"I shouldn't have to tell you. You've been off-planet, Howard, I know you have. You should know better than this. Is beauty all you care about? Haven't you grown?"

"There's no need to be rude. I'm just a man, standing in front of a woman, who he beat up in a cellar... who is beginning to realise how bad that might look if the police arrive."

She nodded. "You are catching on. I'm not here to kill him, Howard, no one is. But he has to face the consequences of what he has done."

"But not today," I said. "Today he has green ties and jam to sell."

"No, not today," she agreed, "but soon. Very soon."

And with that she disappeared from the cellar, as if she had never been there, saving me from an extremely difficult decision.

Howard Phillips wrote this story, which explains a lot. He hopes to one day publish a complete and unexpurgated edition of his novels, so he should really finish writing them.

This Alien I

Antonella Coriander

"Thank the seven stars of the Sistornian system that's over," exclaimed Vorta, impatiently disconnecting herself from the intercisor. "If I ever have to enter the humanoids' cybernet again it'll be too soon." She swung her tail down from the bed and used it to lift herself to the ground. Carefully, of course. She had a baby to think about. Looking down at the size of the swelling beneath her tail, she began to wonder how long they had been under this time.

Barra hadn't said anything yet, so Vorta plodded over to her bed. Aw! She was still sleeping, her rough green tongue lolling peacefully out of her snout. It seemed a shame to wake Barra, but it wasn't a true sleep. She wasn't resting. She was plugged into the incisor, the machine which had translated their consciousnesses into the internet.

"Wake up, sleepyhead!" said Vorta, patting her colleague on the shoulder with the nine claws of her right hand. "We need to get going!"

Barra shifted uneasily in her sleep, and Vorta decided to leave her for a minute or two more.

"Computer!" she roared. "How have you been?"

"Very well," came the polite reply. "Was your mission successful?"

"I think so," said Vorta. "It was confusing at times. There was something odd going on with the cyberweb, and for a while I think we were shunted into robotic humanoid forms. I forgot who I was for a while. It's good to be back in my own scaly skin! How long has it been?"

"Six Earth weeks," replied the ship's computer.

"Whoa! No wonder my little one is no longer so little!"

"I have of course been monitoring the status of your infant, and her progress is excellent. My prediction is that she will emerge into your underpouch within the week."

Vorta snarled with pleasure. "Excellent. Barra is a wonderful colleague, and there isn't a single intelligence officer back on Haddis that I'd have brought in her place. But she can be awfully serious. It'll be nice to have a little chum to play with on the way back. Though I must say, the way I'm being stretched in all the wrong places right now makes me wish we hadn't stopped laying eggs."

The computer didn't understand that she was simply having a grumble. "The survival rate of the younglings of your species has increased by over 3500% in the century since the minor genetic modifications in question."

"Tell it to my spleen, which is currently getting kicked by that minor modification!" She took a few deep breaths and waited for the little devil to calm down. "Computer, could you pour me a drink, please? It's been too long."

A hatch in the wall slid aside to reveal a flagon of Haddissy beer. "Enjoy your drink, captain. But I assure you that I've kept you hydrated throughout your time in the cybernet."

"I'm sure you did, totally sure. Now let's wake Barra. We need to get ready for the return home."

She buried her snout in the flagon and sucked up near half of the beer. In your culture, you might consider this unusual behaviour for a pregnant woman. Things are rather different on Haddis, where beer is an essential nutrient for the skeletal growth of their young. Humans have beer bellies. Haddisses have beer skeletons.

"Withdrawing monitors," announced the computer, as the clips and cables disconnected themselves from Barra and withdrew back into the incisor. "She still isn't waking up."

"Should I be worried?" asked Vorta.

"Try giving her a hug. The contact might encourage her to reconnect with her physical form."

It was hardly appropriate behaviour for a ship's captain! Nevertheless, it seemed necessary. She walked over to Barra's bed. She was still unconscious, though there were signs she was fighting her way back from oblivion. Her eyeshields could not conceal the movement of the eyeballs beneath, her magnificently sturdy legs were bending slightly at the second knee, and the claws of both hands were flexing.

Vorta put a hand on the bed to steady herself, and then leant over to give the required hug. It wasn't entirely unpleasant. She looked forward to hugging her youngling when it finally emerged. "Wake up, Barra," she said, as gently as her larynx would allow.

"Aah, ahh, AH!!" bellowed Barra, her eyes suddenly open and her arms, legs and tail thrashing as if she were caught in a fishing net. "Where am I?"

Her eyes landed on Vorta and her words lost all sense, becoming a meaningless howl of fear.

"Calm down!" ordered Vorta. "I am your captain and I order you to calm down!"

Barra did not seem to be in the mood for following orders. She scrambled to get off the bed and backed into a corner of the room, barely managing to keep herself upright. She held herself still for a moment, let out one more great shout, as if to get it all out of her system, and then said, "What are you? Where am I?"

The computer piped up. "A certain amount of

disorientation is not unusual after long periods using the intercisor."

"I know," said Vorta in a voice dripping with sarcasm. "I have done this before."

"My apologies, captain."

"Shut up!" roared Barra. "Both of you, shut up. Answer my questions! Where am I? What were those three huge statues?"

"I can't shut up and answer your questions," said the computer, irritatingly. "You're usually so much cleverer than this, Commander Barra."

Everyone was silent for a few moments, letting the high feelings ebb somewhat.

Barra broke the silence. "That's not my name."

"That's good to know," said the captain. "What is your name, then?"

"Br– Berz– Baz– Argh!" She smashed her arm against the wall in frustration.

"Doesn't it seem odd," said the computer, "that you cannot say your own name?"

The captain broke in. "The reason is that it wasn't your name, not your real name. You were trying to say B-R-Z-K-9-0-9, weren't you?" Barra nodded.

"That was your designation in the cybernet," said the computer, "not a name ever uttered by a biological entity."

"We sent you in," said Vorta, reaching her claws out in friendship. "But we stayed in too long. You've forgotten who you are. I did too, for a while, but being back on my ship brought it all back."

"I'm... an alien?"

"Well, we don't think of ourselves as aliens! We had a mission, and now we have to return home. I don't know anything about any big statues though. Must have been a glitch in your return journey. Would you like a drink?"

Captain Vorta waved and the computer slid open its

hatch. Not beer, this time, since Barra wasn't pregnant. It was a steaming mug of swamp butter. Barra didn't look very keen.

"Go on, friend. It'll be good for you! Put scales on your chest!"

"I already seem to have scales on my chest," said Borra mournfully.

"That is correct," said the computer. "Haddisses have scales on their chests. I believe the captain is being jocular. You are not the only one who often finds it difficult to tell her jokes from her orders."

Barra tentatively dipped her snout into the swamp butter, and let the drink ripple against her tongue. It was good! It didn't matter at that moment whether this was her real body or not – whatever this body was, it liked that drink! So she drank it right up.

"That's better," said Captain Vorta. "Now, let's freshen up in our quarters – it's been six weeks since either of us had a nice mud bath! – and then meet again in the briefing room. The computer will make sure you don't get lost. There we can discuss our plans, and if you're still struggling with your memory I can answer all your questions. Does that sound okay?"

Barra wasn't at all sure. But she trusted Vorta, for some reason. "Were you Veronique, in the cyberweb?"

"Yes, that's it! It's starting to come back, eh? Thanks for getting me out of that dratted webnoid!"

With that the captain left, muttering something about needing a good long time in the bowel evacuation chamber, and Barra was left alone.

Well, alone except for the computer.

"Computer, where are my quarters?"

"Just a short walk, don't worry. I imagine it's taking you a little while to get used to those legs. So many knees! At least compared to the human suit you were wearing! Just follow the blinking yellow light on the wall. Can you see it?"

"Yes. It's a bit bright. I have a headache."

"Oh, that's not surprising after six weeks in the incisor," said the computer, with a sympathetic tone. "I can do a nice dark shade of purple for you. Is that better?"

"Much better, thank you." Every word was a struggle not to bite her own tongue. She ran a claw across her teeth. They'd be useful if she needed to give someone an injury. Less so if she wanted to bite her nails. She looked at the nine claws on her hands. Perhaps biting them would not be a good idea.

They looked like they would bite back.

She followed the blinking light out of the room. After the plainness of the "dreaming room" (the computer called it) the luxurious decor of the rest of the ship came as a great surprise. The computer explained that the dreaming room was kept plain to prevent any distracting features from making their way into the subject's subconscious. That did not apply to the rest of the ship. Haddisses liked to travel in style. The floors of even the corridors were panelled with wood, as were the walls up to the halfway point. The top half was a rich red velvet, thin enough for the purple blinking light and other displays to shine through it. One could in theory, the computer told her, stop at any point in the ship and use a wall as a command centre.

"And we're the only two Haddisons on board?"

"Haddisses. Yes. I'm here to look after you, and the ship has been doing nothing but sit waiting for your consciousnesses to return to your bodies. Other crew members would have been redundant. Here are your quarters." A door slid aside, accompanied by what sounded like the ringing of a dozen tiny bells. "I have taken the liberty of preparing a nice warm mud bath."

"And I like warm mud baths, do I?"

"I do hope so. We brought the mud all the way from Haddis. It would be a shame to see it go to waste."

Borra did like warm mud baths. In fact, she liked them so much that she worried Captain Vorta would grow impatient waiting for her to arrive at the briefing room. However, Captain Vorta appreciated a warm mud bath just as much, and arrived in the briefing room shortly after Borra, smelling sweetly of the beach puddles of Crawdor, the smallest but warmest continent on Haddis. (Borra wondered how she knew any of that.) Each of them had an immense sofa to lounge on, and the computer kept them well provided with drinks and food.

Oh, the food!

Each time a new plate appeared in front of Borra, the part of her that remembered being Brzk909 (and Beatrice, before that?) turned away in revulsion. Her new body, though, rubbed its claws together and licked its teeth, and she invariably concluded each dish with the belch that signified she had eaten it too quickly. There were plates of lizardly legs, and bowls of squirming insects, and bundles of yellow reeds, and it was all delicious.

While they ate, they talked.

"Overall," said Captain Vorta, picking a wing out of her teeth, "I think the mission has been a success. We successfully penetrated the defences of the cyberweb, and have shown that we can pass undetected long enough to do some damage, if we need to. What did you learn from that data spike?"

The memories were distant and confused, as if they were memories of a dream. In a way, Borra supposed they were. "I made contact with the data spike just as we were being attacked. It explained why I had interfered with my own data tower."

"You had remembered the truth about yourself. About your mission on behalf of Haddis. And once that realisation was recorded in your data tower, there was a risk that others would find out."

"Exactly. And so I set it to quietly delete itself the next time I was out on a mission."

The captain raised an appreciative claw. "An alibi. Clever!"

Borra bared her teeth gratefully. "I then deleted my personal records of the day's events, even the files in which I realised my true mission, so that there wouldn't be anything suspicious for anyone else to find."

"Good, good! I would guess that your final job was to come and find me, and you found a way to have yourself assigned to the most likely place. It was your intelligence rather than luck which brought us back together."

Borra nodded. "I think so, captain."

"And the data spike? Why up on Faben-Dah-237a's tower?"

The computer butted in. "I think I can explain, captain. Borra knew that upon returning from the slow world she would visit her backup. Her backup gone, she would become suspicious. She predicted that she would climb the neighbouring data tower to search for clues, and thus left the spike at the top."

"That sounds very likely," said Borra. "Though I am still struggling to believe I was a Haddissy spy all along. I always felt such a sense of purpose in my work."

"That is your nature," growled the captain. "Had you been added to the cybernet as a tenth-level defragmenter, you would have performed those duties with pride." She sighed, an uncharacteristic sound that from her throat sounded more like the rattling of a bag of seashells. "That was a good life she had, Faben-Dah-237a."

"She rubbed off on me too, Captain Vorta."

"Perhaps your trip to Earth was not just about gathering intelligence," suggested the computer in a tone that suggested it thought itself rather wise. "Perhaps it was also about making friends. Before it is too late."

"Poppycock!" said the captain angrily, waving all eighteen claws in the computer's hypothetical direction.

They ate quietly for a few Earth minutes. Whether it was to calm down, or to avoid the conversation taking that direction, I can't say. (Well, I could, but I choose not to, for the sake of dramatic tension. None of these people are much of a mystery to a genius of my calibre!)

"The last action of the data spike," said Borra, two plates of borgon rashers later, "was to send us back here."

"And just in time too," said Vorta. "They had us bang to rights."

Borra paused for a moment, and then said, "What I still don't understand is this. Us. Back here. Is this real?"

"Feels real enough to me!" shouted Captain Vorta, running her hand over the couch – and inadvertently tearing a hole in it.

"Let me get that," said the computer quietly – this was clearly one of its regular duties!

A small rodent-like device emerged from one corner and leapt upon the hole, stitching it up and then leaving. Now Borra knew what to look for, she saw similar stitching everywhere, on both couches, on the walls. And the panelling of the floor bore a hundred patches too. The price of luxury when it clashes with your claws!

"It will take you a while to adjust," explained the captain. "You haven't used the incisor before, and it takes a lot out of you. When we get back to Haddis—"

Borra leapt to her feet. "Back to Haddis!? We're leaving Earth?!"

"Of course we are. Borra, this isn't our world. We have to go home."

It was almost too much for the junior officer. She was still getting used to her new reptilian form, and now to learn she would be leaving her home planet forever? Maybe it was too much! She sat back down, telling herself that, if this was all true, Earth was not her home planet. Haddis was. She would have to get used to that.

The captain continued, "When we get back to Haddis, there will be plenty to knock your memories back in shape. Old haunts, old friends, that kind of thing. We'll report back to the Great Egg, and then prepare for the invasion."

"The invasion of Earth?"

"Don't be silly," said the captain with a growling laugh. "Why would we want to invade Earth? Granted, its indigenous species looked delicious, but hardly worth all that bother. And there are hardly any decent swamps. No, Earth is planning to invade Haddis. And we must stop them."

As Borra tried to take that in, the captain groaned in pain and slumped back onto the sofa. "Aaaargghh!" she roared. "That really hurts!"

"What is it?" asked Borra, crossing quickly to her side. "Can I help?"

"Do not worry, Commander Borra," said the computer, extending a long metal arm from the floor to rest an ice-pack on the captain's forehead. "The captain is pregnant, and I would guess that the little one is emerging into her underpouch."

"Emerging, you call it!" The captain was practically screaming. "Bursting! Ripping! Exploding! More like."

"Take deep breaths," urged the computer. "My records suggest that this is a painful but brief process."

Borra held the captain's claws. "I'm here for you, Captain Vorta. If there's anything I can do..?"

"Beer, and lots of it!"

The commander kept her superior officer well supplied with alcohol while the youngling made its way into the pouch.

"Four strong knees on this one!" said the captain after one particularly long bout of screaming.

(No apologies for lingering at this point in my narrative. After all the trouble they have caused me, I always take great pleasure in thinking of V&B in pain.)

At last it was over, and the captain, despite her best intentions, closed her eyes and headed for slumberland. She had one question first: "Can you see her? How does she look?"

The captain's underpouch wriggled to the movements of its new occupant, who, having established that the captain was at rest (and thus the environs must be relatively safe), ever so slowly peeked out to see what was what. If she had still been in a human slow suit, Borra would have cried at the cuteness. As it was, she discovered, her body's reaction was to steam from the nostrils at the end of her snout. That could easily be misinterpreted, she thought.

The new arrival was tiny, the head peeking out from the pouch no bigger than a swamp potato. Her snout was still short, and her long ears were stuck to the top of her head by the goo that had assisted her emergence into the underpouch.

"Hi there," said Borra, with all the gentleness this body could muster. "She's lovely, Captain Vorta. Adorable. A chip off the old block."

Vorta still couldn't get her eyes open, but she

managed to say "Not so much of the old!" before dropping off to sleep. Unsurprisingly, the youngling was exhausted too, and having seen what she could see she dropped back into the underpouch, there to sleep, and, in the long term, continue to grow until she would be big enough to make her own way in the world.

After making sure they were comfortable, Borra slid away to the door. She would have preferred to tiptoe, but that would have been ambitious in any new body, and especially so in this one!

Outside, she breathed a sigh of relief and tried to take stock. Which led to staring at the wall and letting her sense of utter bewilderment have its moment.

"If you aren't busy," interrupted the computer, "I have a job you could be doing."

It led her to a corridor which ended in an airlock hatch. Beside it was a rack of spacesuits.

"Put one on, please," said the computer, and, though Borra was slightly concerned by the number of patches on them, she did so. The computer's voice now came from inside her helmet: "Don't be concerned by the repairs – these spacesuits were build with Haddissy use in mind. Scratch them in one place and it only affects that cell – the rest is safe. Safest spacesuits in the galaxy, ours!"

The hatch opened and Borra climbed out onto the spaceship's surface. They were already in deep space – she hadn't realised they had already left Earth. Doubtlessly it had been done that way to give her time to adjust. Well, she had one doubt: what if they had left unannounced to give her no time to prevent it? No time to escape, no time to warn Earth? The spaceship itself was not huge – imagine a row of four terraced houses laid flat on its back.

"Take a seat," suggested the computer. "Your entire suit is magnetized, and the entire ship is surrounded by an energon safety net, so you are in no danger whatsoever."

The seat, Borra saw, was a beautifully upholstered armchair built into the spaceship's superstructure.

She sat in it – it was like a cuddle for her tail! – and out of the ship swung a steering wheel, accelerator and brake pedals, a gear stick and an electronic space map.

"You want me to drive," said Borra incredulously. "Sitting in an armchair on the outside of a spaceship? This is madness!"

"It's the Haddissy way!" said the computer, which sounded slightly offended. "What's the point of travelling in space if you don't make it fun!"

It had a point, thought Borra. The Haddisses seemed to have a good attitude to life. She took hold of the steering wheel with all eighteen claws and put her foot down on the accelerator.

If Borra had seen Rassisi – the capital city of Haddis – before, her brain didn't seem to know it. Her brain was as agog as her eyes. It was an astonishing sight. And confusingly, she couldn't tell whether she liked it or not. On a logical, rational level she was convinced that she found it rather repulsive. But on a physical, visceral level she loved it.

Don't think of one of your human cities. This wasn't a pile of big brick and concrete buildings jammed into a space far too small. Those are magnificent in one way. Rassisi was magnificent in another. It had grown at the mouth of the largest river on the planet, the Elin, stretching from one bank to the other, four kilometres away, and then unfurling up the river for almost thirty kilometres.

Every inhabitant of Rassisi had easy access to the river, and was able to drop in for a swim or a bask whenever the mood took them. That they invariably emerged from the river caked in glorious mud explained the dirtiness of each building's exterior.

As Borra (with a bit of help from the computer) brought their ship in to land, she could see them doing just that. A terrifying sight for the part of her that remembered thinking she was the human Beatrice, an intriguing sight for the part of her that had thought itself the computer program Brzk909, and a welcome sight for Commander Borra of the Haddissy Space Fleet.

They were here to visit the Great Egg, and there it was, five storeys high, supported by a scaffold of tree trunks. The Haddisses loved their luxury, but they did not build to last. To them, a building that would not rot was an abomination. There was nothing so lovely to them as being able to dig into the walls of their homes and claw out some delicious worms and beetles! The joy of a home that was no longer habitable was that the construction of a new abode would provide useful employment to other Haddisses.

This philosophy did not extend to the spaceport, which was for practical reasons built upon dry land, its layer of ironcrete suppressing the vegetation. A necessary evil, all agreed, once they knew of Earth's plans to invade.

Much of this was explained to Borra by the computer as they came in to land. It was peculiar to have that calm voice chattering in her helmet as she rode a spaceship down to the ground.

"Quite a ride!" exclaimed Borra once they were down.

"I thought you would enjoy it," said the computer. "Let's go down and wake Captain Vorta and the youngling. They may appreciate your help in disembarking."

"Of course," said Borra, getting out of her armchair. Now they were in the grip once more of gravity, the magnetising of her spacesuit became a bit of a bother. She slipped out of it and carried it back down into the airlock.

"You managed not to tear it?" said the computer.

Borra turned it over for a look. "Not as far as I know. Maybe I'm getting used to these claws."

A knock on the captain's door provoked an angry growl and a high-pitched squeal.

"I think they're awake," said Borra.

She helped the captain, after a quick drink of swamp butter each, to leave the ship. Normally Vorta would have swung down the ladder like Curious Georgina. With the baby on board she took it more slowly, curling her tail around the rungs with each step down.

"Good luck!" called the computer from above.

Maybe this wasn't the first time Borra had set foot on an alien planet, and maybe this wasn't even an alien planet for her, but it felt like it was. At that moment she had never felt more like Beatrice, even if, in her heart, she knew Beatrice had been nothing but a two-time lie. The blue sky of Earth had never been appreciated more, as she looked up at a green sky streaked with purple. Bright and colourful, but it made her tummy feel funny.

A cheerful Haddis with short legs and an unusually long tail ran across the concrete to them. "Captain Vorta! Commander Borra! You have returned!" She noticed the adorable little head poking out from the captain's underpouch. "And you have brought back this incredible cuteness with you!" She began reaching out to pet the youngling, but a growl from the captain warned her off.

"My apologies," said Borra. "I am suffering from memory problems after spending so long in the incisor. I don't remember your name."

"I understand completely – a very common problem, I believe. I am Flight Commander Zigglesward. I was

present at your briefing, but haven't known you long."
Zigglesward began to lead them towards the river. "We
have a boat waiting to take you straight to the Great
Egg. Tell me, though: was the mission a success?"

Borra looked at the captain. "I think so. I have to
admit, I'm not completely sure what it was."

"Quite normal, Commander Borra. Quite normal!"

The captain spoke up. "Yes, Zigglesward. The
mission was a success. We infiltrated the human
cybernet. Destroyed data storage. Escaped with our
lives. Drank some beer. Gave birth to a youngling."

"Terrific!" said Flight Commander Zigglesward. "Do
you think we will be able to prevent the human
invasion?" They had reached the river bank, and she
helped Vorta and Borra down into the boat. Knees,
elbows and tails were everywhere. Haddisses rarely
used boats, preferring at all times to swim where
possible. The time spent on Earth in the incisor, and
then in space, and the recent birth of the captain's
youngling, made the boat necessary. Space travellers
had been known to sink straight to the bottom upon
their return to the river.

Still, there was no need to separate themselves
entirely from their natures, and Zigglesward and Vorta
used their tails to paddle the boat in the right
direction. Borra joined in, once she realised what they
were doing, paddling her tail first on one side, then
the other, so that she didn't spin them in a circle.
Vorta's youngling stared at everything with the
mingled joy and fear of the very young when
encountering the unknown. Borra understood how she
felt.

"Impossible to say," said the captain at last. "As far as
I could tell, the inhabitants of the cybernet, and
beyond that the human world, were completely
unaware of the invasion plans."

Zigglesward nodded her head, and gave a tiny growl

of dissatisfaction. "Being able to access the cybernet is undoubtedly useful, but it will only be useful to the extent that the invaders actually use it."

"I have no knowledge of an invasion from Earth," said Borra. "Except from what you two have told me."

"Well, we are sure it is coming," said Zigglesward sadly. "The Great Egg has told us so."

As they paddled past the houses, receiving cheery waves from wallowing Haddisses, Borra began to get a sense of just how Great the Egg was. It towered over everything else – at no point was it ever blocked entirely from their sight. The framework around it looked awfully rickety, but Zigglesward assured her that that was how they liked it.

"If the Egg was at no risk, where would be the pride in keeping it safe?" she said. "We can't spend all day swimming, you know! Much as we would like to!"

Captain Vorta and the Flight Commander laughed heartily. This was a favourite joke among the Haddisses, who did after all spend a good portion of each day in the water.

It might have been her imagination, but it seemed to Borra that the captain was very glad to be back home. It could hardly have been easy, having a youngling in deep space, far from the tasty squid of home.

Getting out of the boat was as much of a palaver as getting into it. But there they were: standing on a boardwalk that ran around the base of the Great Egg! The slightest inclination on its part would have crushed them – and a good part of the city. Borra wondered what would happen next. Would they talk to the Great Egg itself? She cleared her throat just in case – alarming the youngling!

But no, they were to go inside the Great Egg. A segment tall enough for them to pass through lowered itself onto the boardwalk.

Zigglesward took the lead. Vorta and Borra followed.

The noisiness of the Great Egg's interior came as a shock after the tranquillity of Rassisi. It thundered with the echoed footfalls of Haddisses as they ran around, tending first one computer display, then another. Though the outer shell of the Great Egg had been plain, blemished only by splashes of mud and the tracks of the rain, the inner side was criss-crossed with embedded electronics. Above her head she could see a profusion of platforms, blocking her view in some directions but allowing it in others, apparently climbing to the Great Egg's very peak.

Zigglesward noticed her curiosity. "The Great Egg has been nurtured for a hundred Haddissy years, and continues to grow. It is a living computer, drawing power and inspiration from its own inner lining."

"And the yolk?" asked Borra.

"That's where we're going," growled the captain. "Watch yourself. The Great Egg is tasked with looking after all of us. Not each of us."

They climbed from one platform to another by means of spiralling staircases, and Borra tried not to think of the consequences should she slip. Other Haddisses would rely on their tail should they fall – she wasn't sure she was adept enough in its use to rely on it just yet.

At last they reached the uppermost platform, their ascent delayed by questions, congratulations and greetings. Flight Commander Zigglesward did her best to keep them moving, though Borra could tell she was enjoying her small share in their small glory.

No other Haddisses stood on the uppermost platform. It was just the three of them. Borra corrected herself: the four of them. She had forgotten the youngling. She was about to ask Captain Vorta if she had decided upon a name, when the Great Egg spoke to them.

"Captain Vorta," it boomed. All activity in the Great Egg came to an immediate halt. Every Haddis in the place turned to listen. "Commander Borra. Your mission has been a success. You have travelled to Earth and infiltrated the human cybernet. As I predicted."

"Thank you, Great Egg," said Captain Vorta. "We were glad to perform this duty."

"Your duty is not over," boomed the Great Egg. "Now one of you, armed with that knowledge of the human world, must lead our people in the defence of this planet. We must decide which."

"It should be Captain Vorta," blurted Borra. "She is my superior, and I am experiencing memory problems."

"Those problems do not concern me," boomed the Egg. "They may even prove beneficial. You still think like a human. Nor do the ranks you have attained concern me. This is too important for that."

Borra and Vorta looked at Flight Commander Zigglesward, who simply shrugged.

"No," continued the Great Egg. "That is not how it shall be done. There shall be a fight. A fight to the death."

Antonella Coriander has never been happier. "This Alien I" is the sixth episode of her ongoing Oulippean serial, Les aventures fantastiques de Beatrice et Veronique.

The Stone Gods of Superspace

Howard Phillips

I. The Castaways of Time

I awoke. Where was I? Mere moments before I, Howard Phillips, writer, poet, adventurer, had been... what? In Pierre's silly shop, looking at the label on a jar of broccoli jam. A label showing three huge statues, against a mad background of shooting stars. Had an assassin struck during that moment, and this was my heaven? I don't know why I'm asking you, you probably don't know. You're reading this to find out!

I opened my eyes, to see the background of that same label above me, streaks of stars across the sky, whirling past in some mad helter-skelter dash for parts unknown. Seen in motion these clearly weren't meteorites, and real stars don't move like that. More likely I was on something that was spinning. Surely not a planet, at this speed? A space station? A ship? And I was seeing space through a viewport? Yet my hands lay in sand, or dry dirt.

No more information was to be had from my current position. I decided to sit up, and after my brain had a few angry conversations with various bits of my body, it happened.

All thoughts of establishing my location were

abandoned immediately, because to my left and right were two beautiful women. Of course, all women are beautiful, each of them a magnificent and unique creation whose individual existence is so remarkably improbable that we should treasure them all. So there is some redundancy in saying that there were two beautiful women, but to my eyes these were particularly marvellous examples of the human species.

When I look in the mirror, I see the pallid, lifewrecked, desiccated face of Howard Phillips, eyes marooned behind thick glasses, lips as dry as an Arctic desert. Should it come as such a surprise, then, that I enjoy so much the sight of beauty? One had a small round face, with many colours in her hair. Her eyes darted beneath her lids. The other had a look of unstoppable determination, even unconscious. If my heart had not already been preoccupied with Pierre Samuels, there's a good chance I would have lost it twice over in that moment.

"Hello?" I spoke gently, to wake them. Reaching out might be unwise. If they woke like me, confused and concerned, they might take me for their captor and lash out. Each looked formidable in her own way. "Are either of you awake? I mean, I know that you aren't, but would you like to wake up? Because I don't know where I am, and I don't know how I got here, and I'm hoping you might be able to help."

The more I talked, the more they stirred, and at last the woman with only one colour in her hair opened her eyes. She looked at the stars, then looked at me, then looked at the other woman, then back at me again. She seemed as startled by me as by anything else.

"Hello," she said slowly.

"Hi." I smiled, in what I hoped was not a thoroughly

creepy way. It is difficult with a face like mine. "I'm Howard. Howard Phillips. Poet, musician, adventurer."

She pushed herself up on to her elbows and stared at me for a minute. "Howard. That's an... unusual name."

"Not so much where I'm from," I replied. "There's me, for starters. And the regular cover artist of Theaker's magazine is called Howard too. Then there's H.P. Lovecraft, of course."

She looked me queerly. "Harriet Lovecraft?"

"Not where I'm from."

"Hm. So it would seem we are not from the same place."

I smiled, in what I hoped would seem a friendly way. "What's your name, if you don't think it rude?"

"Beatrice," she said. Then thought for a minute. "Yes, Beatrice. But that wasn't my name before. I was Barra. I wasn't even human. I was a computer program or something. Called Brzk909." She put her hands to her face, stroked her cheeks, then dug her hands into her abdomen, almost as if she were rooting around for something. "Yes, human now. Not a program. Not a robot. And all in one piece. Haven't been burned to a crisp or anything."

I decided to give her a bit of time to calm down, and turned my attention to the other woman, who was waking up too, albeit with much more reluctance. It gave me the impression that this young woman did not generally get enough sleep, and her body was glad of the opportunity.

"Are you okay?" I asked, when she managed to force her eyes open. They burned at me like tiny volcanoes, then gave up and closed once more.

"Yes," she said, taking deep breaths and tapping the ground with her fingers in a funny little beat. "I'm fine. But wherever you've brought me, I don't have time to be here. I was at an important banquet. They had just brought out my food."

"I'm sorry your meal was interrupted. I don't know how I got here either. I'm Howard Phillips," I declared, "a traveller, a singer and an experiencer of life at its fullest. What's your name?"

"Have you heard of Zeddy Graves?" she asked.

I had not, so I shook my head.

"Then I'm Zeddy Graves. I too am a musician!"

I wondered, was that what this was? My exploits with the Saturation Point, the greatest band in all of time and space, were now the stuff of legend, a matter of history. But had someone forgotten to tell the universe, and it was still trying to bring me together with new bandmates, in new adventures?

Of course not, that couldn't be it. It hadn't been the universe, anyway, it hadn't been fate, it hadn't been destiny, or the gods, or the muses. I shuddered to remember who it had been. Ugh!

Beatrice had got to her feet and was looking from left to right, hand raised to shield her eyes from what I now realised was a dim but persistent sun. No hull or cloud or building blocked us from its light. We seemed to be in a dimple, perhaps a kilometre wide, that gave us an unbroken, featureless horizon. Above us, the spinning stars, around us, a pinkish gravel. We were, so far, the most interesting things in this place.

"What do we have?" said Beatrice. "We have our clothes. But do we have water, food, tools, weapons? My pockets are empty. How about yours?"

I checked, and then shook my head. "I have my squared moleskine and a Muji gel pen. That's it. Sorry."

The woman calling herself Zeddy Graves slapped herself on the hip, and rolled her face in disappointment when nothing happened. "Nothing here, either."

"And none of you know how we got here?" asked Beatrice. "Nothing at all?"

"I was in a shop," I said. "Looking at jam jars. Hoping someone would fall in love with me. I thought maybe I was knocked on the head and abducted. It wouldn't be the first time. And there were assassins on the prowl."

Beatrice took a long, hard look at Zeddy Graves, who met her eyes for exactly as long as it took for each to know she could never trust the other. But Zeddy did answer. "I don't know how we got here. It wasn't me. I was surrounded by dangerous people at the time, though. Any one of them could be responsible."

She had a nervous energy that made me wary of her, and yet I thought she was telling the truth. My impression was that she liked to be in control, and she seemed uncomfortable with the current situation.

"Okay," said Beatrice, taking charge of the situation, and neither Zeddy nor I were in the mood to quarrel about it, "we need to move. Whatever this place is, there's nothing here to eat or drink. And whoever – or whatever – brought us here, this is where they'll expect to find us. We should move."

"Together?" I asked.

We both looked at Zeddy, who glared back with unsuppressed irritation. "Together," she hissed. "What else?"

She reached out and grabbed my hand. I let myself be led away. Looking back over my shoulder, I saw Beatrice frowning, and then trotting after us. One direction was as good as any other, till we had the lay of the land.

The stars continued to spin.

As we walked I felt Zeddy tapping a beat on the back of my hand. It wasn't Morse code, though I waited long enough to be absolutely sure. Then I began to tap back, the high-hat to her four-to-the-floor. If she could have seen our faces, Beatrice would have wondered why we had begun to smile. It was something to do. Zeddy pulled me along slightly faster than I'd have gone on my own – one never knows what'll be hiding over the top of the ridge, how much running you'll need to do, how much fighting, how much impromptu performance art. And indeed we didn't know, we couldn't have known, but we should probably have taken more care, just in case.

"What the heck?" said Beatrice, when we saw what lay beyond that ridge.

They were far off in the distance, we knew that because there was so much else between them and us, canyons and mountains and deserts and rivers, but that was impossible, because if they were so far away that meant that they must be... Had to be... It was only logical... Incredibly huge. Gargantuan. Brobdingnagian.

The three statues I had seen on the jamjar. There they were. Not an image, not a replica, but real, and right there, looming over the land like grim tired parents over a naughty baby's cot. Two male figures. One female, in a demonic black dress.

They turned to face us.

And opened their black eyes.

"I think that's where we're going," I said.

The sky went yellow behind them, as if afraid of what it saw.

II. Flight Through a Forest

"That pit we just came out of," said Beatrice, shock in her voice. "I think it's a footprint."

I turned to look back down the ridge. From our new

position we could see the shape cut out of the surrounding forest, and it did, indeed, resemble nothing so much as the outline of an immense foot, one that had stamped down hard enough to disintegrate everything beneath it.

"That level of destruction..." said Zeddy Graves, almost dumbstruck. "It's incredible."

"Awful," said Beatrice, provoking a hurried nod of agreement from Zeddy. I rather thought she had meant it when she had said incredible. "Whatever those things are, they did this. Look out there." She pointed out in their direction. We could see other footprints along the way, immense and portentous. Some were like this one, utterly desolate. Others were different. One looked like a fence surrounded it, though at such a distance I could have been mistaken. Another, very far off, glittered blue, but perhaps that was just a lake. "They passed this way. Caused all this havoc."

"Then called us here," said Zeddy.

Beatrice and I looked at her. "How do you mean?" asked Beatrice.

Zeddy pointed at me. "He saw these statues on a jamjar. He said so. I saw them too. On a dinner tray. I think they brought us here. They need us. Our help."

Beatrice looked doubtful.

"You don't remember them?" I asked.

She shook her head, but then her eyes took on a faraway look, and settled on the three statues, who stared right back. "Maybe," she said. "You've got to understand, things have been pretty weird for me lately. Last I remember, I was coming out of a computer system or something. And maybe then, maybe I saw something. Nothing I've seen lately has made any sense."

I nodded. "I think we all have that in common."

"That's why they chose us," said Zeddy with enthusiasm. "Experience."

I looked again at Beatrice. "Do you have any musical experience?"

She looked at me like I was mad. "What's that got to do with anything?"

I shrugged. "I was in a band. Zeddy is a musician, and a good one too if I know my stuff. I thought maybe that might be the connection."

Beatrice shook her head. "I've had lessons, but that's not what I do for a living. I'm a police officer. I was pursuing a thief across the channel when we both got caught up in a storm. And I haven't been home since then."

"And now you're no closer," I said. "The stars are moving pretty fast, but I don't think this is Earth. I don't think we have many options but to go on. Whether those things brought us here or not, and whatever they want, staying here will do us no good. I propose we make our way in their direction, at first heading for the footprint with the fence."

Beatrice nodded. "A fence needs builders. If they look dangerous, we avoid them. If not, they could help us. We could learn something, at least."

Though the idea of walking closer to those statues under the weight of their dreadful stares filled me with horror, it was the best option. What could we hope to find in any other direction? If the fence surrounded a town or settlement, then at least I might find somewhere to sit down and compose a poem or two. Thank goodness for my moleskine. Even torn away from my own world I had the power to create new works of art!

We began to make our way down through the woods, and the going soon became very difficult. The statues, of course, had left no trail for us to follow, the gaps between each of their footfalls too huge to clear our route, and the trees soon blocked the statues themselves entirely from our sight. The spinning of the stars gave us little to go on except the direction of rotation, and even that was only when we could make them out through the ever-thickening canopy. I was not even certain that the spinning was in a consistent direction. Who could tell on this higgledy-piggledy world?

Soon we were pushing our way under and over interlocking branches, sneaking through the slow-motion battle of a thousand trees for sunlight and water and territory. We tried not to damage them as we passed, but if they appreciated our discretion they did nothing to show it, cramming closer and closer together until they felt more like lovers than enemies. At the height of my discomfort, at the depth of the darkness, at the point where I knew not if we were heading in the right direction at all, there came a cry, and then another cry, and then twenty cries.

I heard fear, and glee, and anger, and vengeance in those cries, and so did my companions of the moment. It made Zeddy laugh. "It's all about to happen!" She was right. Beatrice and I knew it.

"Not far to go," said the police officer. "We can do this. If we can get out of these woods, we can get away. We can get to the fence."

I didn't believe her for a second, but it was enough that she wanted me to believe, and I kept struggling and pushing through, not caring now if I broke branches, or if they slapped me in the face, or if I had to rip off leaves to pull myself through. I was covered in sap from head to toe, a horticulturalist's nightmare, the green stuff running down my back like it was my own sweat, the cries and howls coming ever closer.

And then the cries were ahead of us, and they turned to whoops as the hunters laid eyes on us and we laid eyes on them. It was as if the woods chose that moment to revenge themselves upon us, the canopy opening up for a brief moment, not long enough to help us find our way, but long enough to let us be discovered.

I wriggled out from the tree in whose embrace I was currently locked, and held up a hand in peace. There were three of them. Humanoid, but not, so far as I could tell, human, unless there had been substantial mutation or evolution in their past. Their earlobes were long, reaching almost to the floor. At first I thought this an evolutionary adaptation that was unlikely to be of assistance in forest life, but it wasn't long before my mistake was revealed. Their noses came not to a point, instead continuing up to arc back into their foreheads, six nostrils along their lengths like the suckers on an octopus's tentacle. Their skin was a dark purple, their hands, so far as you'd call them that, full of sharp-looking weapons. There were no guns, and at least that was something, but a pointy stick in the guts leaves you no less dead than a bullet in the same place.

"We don't want to fight you," I said, hoping that they would understand. Their response was simply to viciously snarl, and then whoop at the heavens to attract the attention of their fellows. I tried again in other languages I had learnt in my travels to the end of the universe and beyond, but whether I tried the language of Envia or that spoken in Ban Village the result was the same.

"It's no good, Howard," said Zeddy Graves. "There's no time. We have to get past them before it's too late." She moved quickly in their direction, flitting from shadow to shadow as if she were a trick of the light.

"Wait!" said Beatrice, but the fight had already begun, and there was nothing to do but join our new-found comrade in the fray.

None of we three were armed. At first, anyway.

Zeddy danced around our opponents, dashing in to slice with the nails of one hand while snatching at weapons with the other. It wasn't long before she was successful, and I found myself with a good strong staff with which I could begin to poke at the biggest of our three enemies. Beatrice declined the offer of a weapon of her own, being content for now to punch her attacker in the nose. Blood poured from all six nostrils.

"Finish them!" hissed Zeddy, staring one in the eyes while tossing a knife from hand to hand.

By this point we had found our way beyond them and could have made our escape. They were not in any condition to pursue. "There's no need," I said. "Let's go." I shook my fist at our attackers and made to leave.

Zeddy shook her head and scowled. "You'll regret it. We need to finish them off or they'll be back."

She went for the closest of them with the knife raised, determined that it would taste blood. That was enough for the attackers. They threw their earlobes up into the trees and pulled themselves up, up and away.

"Cowards," said Zeddy, sneering in their direction.

"Now it's our turn," said Beatrice. "Their friends are almost here."

We ran for it, or as close to it as the forest would allow. Luckily, the three members of the advance guard must have chosen that spot for their ambush because it was where the trees began to open out, and we took full advantage. Though leaves still slapped us and twigs still scratched us, there were fewer of them with each step, and though the three purple warriors still followed at a safe distance, swinging from branch to branch with their elongated lobes, the shouts of the other pursuers began to take on a more plangent quality. They worried that we had escaped them, and we almost had.

"There's the edge of the trees," shouted Beatrice, the

first to spot the breaking light, and we adjusted the direction of our stampede to take us that way.

III. The Fenced Footprint

Our mad dash through the forest had left no time for gathering nuts and berries (though I had sipped on water from leaves when it was possible to do so without breaking my stride) so by the time we reached the next footprint we were extremely tired and extremely hungry. The purple men and women had shied away from chasing us beyond their woodland territory, but three days of walking without food had very nearly done us in anyway.

I knocked again on the gate.

It was one half of my height, and if it ever opened I might have real trouble fitting through. So far that problem had failed to present itself, to our great discomfort.

"Should we try going over the fence?" asked Beatrice, with an air that suggested words prompted by hopelessness rather than a sincere belief in their potential to improve our position.

The fence was five metres high, built of wood so solid that when you knocked it knocked right back, and topped with sharp points. We were in a grassy field. We had no way of getting over, not unless – perhaps! – we tied all our clothes together and tried to chuck it up there. It was a daft idea, but I didn't get this far in life without taking a risk on a few of those.

"Maybe later," I said. "Once it's dark." It had come as a surprise when night fell on this strange place, the first time. I whispered my idea, and they looked at each other with raised eyebrows.

"We're not that desperate," said Zeddy with a sneer. "Pervert."

I stared at them as blankly as a poet asked to kick a football, but didn't protest my innocence. If it was a good idea, they would come around. If it was a bad idea, it was better that they didn't.

Beatrice took a turn to knock, and this time there was a response, a snarling, gruff, quite terrifying response: "What is it?"

Beatrice smiled. Her interlocutor probably couldn't see it, but I've seen people do this before: smiling puts them in the right frame of mind. "We are looking for shelter. We have been walking for three days, fleeing from enemies."

"The wood folk?" said the voice, with undisguised anger.

"Yes," she said. "The wood folk. They attacked us, and we ran. We couldn't see anywhere else to go, so we came here."

The gate opened, and a little girl emerged, a human girl, a gun in one hand, a sword in the other. She couldn't have been more than three years old. She looked each of us up and down in turn, and did not seem that impressed with me. Beatrice smiled and held out a friendly hand, prompting the little girl to raise the sword in warning.

"How do they look, Taio?" called the gruff voice.

The girl stared at us for ten seconds more, then called back. "They seem okay, Dad. No weapons. Let them in."

"Okay," he said, "your call."

The girl darted back in through her little door, which closed behind her. A wider gate now opened, and the three of us went inside.

I don't know what I was expecting, but it wasn't what we found. Rubble stretched as far as the eye could see, spaces cleared here and there to allow the construction of small huts. The largest building we could see, what looked like a tavern or food hall from the people going back and forth to it, stood hard against the far fence, as if huddling to hide from the sight of the statues. Those people were purple and long-lobed, much like those from whom we had fled, yet apparently with less desire to see us dead.

"Welcome to Footprint," said the man who had let us in. His daughter stood at his heel, weapons still in hand. He held nothing, and yet I had no doubt that should he want me dead I would not live long. "It had another name once, but that was crushed, like everything else, when the gods walked past."

"Gods?" I said, with interest. Did this man know where we were? What this place was?

He shrugged. "That's what people think. Gods, statues, aliens. Same difference. One footfall was all it took to destroy this place, and every man, woman and child within it. Those who survived, those who were out in the fields, or travelling, or taking a morning constitutional, split into two groups. Those who have tried to rebuild, and those who worship the statues, and wish to see the destruction of this town complete."

"I think we met them," said Zeddy. "They were not cool."

"Definitely not," said the man, giving her his first smile of the conversation. He reached out to shake her hand, earning a scowl from his daughter. "Introductions, then? Because it doesn't seem like you recognise me. I am Bardello Fatloch."

The name meant nothing to any of us.

"Interesting," he said. "You don't even know my name. I was once a president, but there was some trouble and we had to leave. My daughter Taio and I had been travelling in space for a couple of years, looking for alien civilisations, when suddenly we found ourselves here, right in the middle of one, or at least its remains. We have helped the Omnobisians to build their fence, to fight off the Followers, and to plan for a future which seems extremely uncertain."

I didn't know what to say to that. Parts of his story sounded vaguely familiar, but don't forget, I lived to the end of the universe as we know it and beyond into the facsimile in which we all now live, so *all* stories sound familiar to me. That's just the way it is.

Beatrice took up the conversational slack. "Thank you for letting us inside. It sounds like we have the same enemies. We three arrived on this world suddenly too, just a few days ago. I am Beatrice, a police officer." If his eyes narrowed, she pretended not to notice. "This is Zeddy Graves, a musician and singer. And this is Howard Phillips, a poet and adventurer."

"And also a musican?" said Fatloch. "I know your name. The Sound of Howard Phillips. Howard Phillips and the Saturation Point. All that stuff. Is that you? You made an album... The Fear Man?"

Zeddy Graves seemed put out that my name was recognised while hers was not, but I stared at Fatloch in astonishment. That's where I knew his name. *The Fear Man*. The terrible novel by Theaker that our band had adapted into a concept album. But that was a novel. He couldn't be here, now, wherever here and now was. And how could he have heard an album that was about him?

I decided not to say anything about any of that. It would only confuse matters, and that might get in the way of us eating some food. "Yes, that's me," I said instead.

"It's a good album," he said. "Not your best, but good. Reminded me of myself in some ways." His eyes took on a faraway look, then snapped back to us. Perhaps he went through a mental process similar to mine. "We should get you some food."

The tavern was not a place you'd go to if you had a choice. Rough, splintered and dirty, it was no place for a Sunday dinner with the family. But right then I loved it better than the swankiest restaurant in Paris, the most famous pizzeria in New York, or the best fish and chip shop in Brighton.

There was even a musician in the corner, playing "Helter Skelter" by the Beatles on an upturned cup and bowl. He was another human, called himself Dodge. I tried talking to him, but he wanted nothing to do with us. ("I'm just waiting for Martin to put this timeline right," he said. "Leave me alone.")

There wasn't much good to choose from, but the bread rolls fell into my mouth like teardrops on a wounded heart, and the thick hot soup sang like the sirens of the Scottish highlands. (I must tell you the story of them some day.)

"Thank you," I said to Fatloch between mouthfuls. "If you hadn't let us in, we wouldn't have survived."

"Don't thank me," he said. "I wouldn't have taken the risk. But Taio is a good judge of character. And she doesn't like it when I let good people die." He frowned at his daughter in a fatherly way, and she frowned right back.

The tavern didn't have an owner as such. Rebuilding was at such an early stage that everyone pitched in, but one woman was clearly at the centre of the hustle and bustle, and in a quiet moment she joined us. Her lobes were decorated with a jostle of jewellery, and her eyes burned with the pain of a person who has lost everything but won't give up. I wanted to give her a hug, but it wouldn't have been appropriate.

"This is Jessally Joist," said Fatloch. "She put me to work here."

"We couldn't have anyone better at the gate," she said, putting a hand on his shoulder. He too, I could tell, was in much pain – he shuddered with the effort of accepting the gesture. "What do the three of you plan to do? Can you help us here?"

I looked at Beatrice and Zeddy, both of them eating as enthusiastically as me. We hadn't thought about this question, thought any further than reaching this place and getting to safety. But this wasn't safety, not really, not for long, this was clinging on in the face of incomprehensible power. If one footfall had wreaked such havoc, what could those statues do if they really tried?

"We have to press on," I said, before I had time to reconsider. "It's amazing to see how you're bringing these survivors together to rebuild, but they won't truly be safe until those gods of yours are gone."

"And you think we can do it?" asked Beatrice.

"I don't know," I admitted. I could never have lied to Beatrice. She'd have known it before the words left my lips. "But we can at least gather knowledge about them. Even if it kills us, we might find the clue that brings them down."

"A fact-finding suicide mission," said Fatloch with a grim smile. "I admire your courage."

I smiled. If he knew how much courage it took to take the stage at a poetry slam he would think nothing of this.

"Let's do it," said Zeddy. "I can't stay in this dump for the rest of my life. Offence intended."

Jessally's lobes twitched but did not lash out. "Offence taken," she said.

"I agree with Howard," said Beatrice. "We need more information. We've been pulled here randomly, plucked out of time, perhaps even from different dimensions, different realities, and we don't know why. It must be something to do with these gods. How long have they been here?"

"About three of your Earth years," said Jessally.

"And how come your people speak English?" asked Zeddy.

"How come you can speak Omnobisian?" replied Jessally.

"A babel effect?" Beatrice said. "Interesting. Someone wants us talking to each other."

"When you have slept," Jessally said, "I shall arrange your provisions, lead you from here, set you on your way. But sleep first. You have far to go."

It was not to be that simple. I woke in darkness to the sound of screaming.

IV. Excelsior!

The wood folk were attacking from all sides, a co-ordinated assault, fires set at every point along the fence. Their screams filled the night sky, their lobes flinging darts into our midst. We were fortunate perhaps that they believed their gods to despise technology, hence their return to the woods. If they had been properly armed we would have died in our sleep.

We had been sleeping in Fatloch's hut. It was quite close to the tavern, and he was on night watch. (He seemed to be on every watch, so far as I could tell.) I barely knew Beatrice and Zeddy, but we had bedded down in the same room without any discussion. Nowhere was safe on this world. Together we were possibly an infinitesimal bit safer.

So it had proved. As I woke to screams in darkness, Zeddy was already twisting the lobes of an attacker and forcing him back out of our hut. She gave him a sharp punch in the small of the back and slammed the door, giving Beatrice and me a chance to gather our wits and get to our feet.

Now we were outside, and ready to join the fight.

Fatloch was everywhere at once, clambering up the fence to slash at the head of a would-be intruder, then leaping back in a somersault to land on the head of another who had successfully got in. I must have seen him kill ten of the wood folk before I even engaged with one. He was that good.

And Taio as well. That little girl could fight! The former president had told us of their mission, to find new life and new friends for Earth, and how he had trained her to defend herself, that she might continue the mission safely after his death, but his words had not done her justice. She scampered everywhere in the darkness, like a malicious little goblin, rolling under foot and slicing heels, cutting knees. She didn't kill, which would have been admirable if her actions weren't so dreadful in themselves.

I began to see how this scrappy little community had survived long enough to build its huge fence. The fires set along its length weren't quite taking hold, which was a relief. Patches here and there of dry brush were smoking away, but the bulk of it was untouched, resisting the licking flames like an elderly dog ignoring a puppy playing with her tail.

As we three entered the fight it seemed we might prevail. We found ourselves close by Jessally, who smiled to see us at her side.

"They have attacked before," she cried above the noise, "but never in such numbers."

"They must be after us," I said. "They've followed from the woods."

"Maybe." She shook her head. "No, I don't think so. This isn't rage. This was planned. They want us gone. They think it's a blasphemy against the stone gods to rebuild here. They think it's sacred ground."

"A sacred footprint," said Beatrice, punching a forest woman first in the nose, then on each shoulder, and finally pushing her to the ground to be tied with her own lobes. "People..."

We thought we might prevail... What a joke of fate! A cruel prank! A mischievous shenanigan! For it was at that point that the three statues unleashed their power. Six beams of burning red rays hit Footprint all at once, scouring away sections of fence, incinerating huts and homes, frying the Omnobisians to a crisp before their lobes had even twitched. The skin on my face burned as if I were being roasted on a spit, though I was fortunate to avoid the full power of the death rays. The forest folk leapt in jubilation. So far as I could tell the rays had killed indiscriminately, but that didn't seem to bother them. Perhaps they were just happy to have their beliefs confirmed. More of them now poured in through the newly-opened gaps in the fence.

Jessally was in shock, staring at the new ruination heaped upon her brave town. Then she shook it off, and began pushing us in the direction of the tavern, miraculously still standing. "Get yourselves food and water, then get out of here."

"What about you and your people?" asked Beatrice, even as Zeddy was already halfway to the tavern.

"We can fight off these fools," she said. "Most of their strength was already gone, and we have the advantage of Bardello, Taio and metalwork. But you must go now, while they focus on us, and while the stone gods' power is at its lowest. We have seen them use their death gaze before, on other communities – yet never more than twice in one week. My duty is here, to my people. Yours is to escape from here, to reach the stone gods, and, if you can, destroy them."

"I accept that duty," I said, and we parted with a hug that left me wishing for a sequel.

Beatrice and I joined Zeddy in gathering together enough food for our journey, or at least its early stages.

It was still difficult to judge how far away the stone gods were, but I thought we could be at the next footprint – the one that had become a lake – in three days, and surely there would be fish or fishlike things to eat there. If not, we would have enough bread to keep us going for a few days more.

It was a long trek, and guilt dogged our heels. Mine and Beatrice's, anyway, I don't think Zeddy really cared. At least the ground was easy: long, rolling moors of grass and heather that bounced under our feet, adding a literal spring to our step. Small furry animals darted here and there, too fast for us to catch without putting a lot of time into it. It was good to know they were there should we grow desperately hungry.

We didn't talk much, perhaps unwilling to reflect on what we had left behind. Zeddy whistled to herself, and Beatrice looked like she was assembling and discarding one plan after another as she walked. I didn't interrupt her train of thought: it might be what we rode out of here. My own plans were as shapeless as my formless thoughts. I had very nearly fallen in love with Jessally, as is my wont, and probably would have done were it not for my unbreakable crush on the glorious Pierre Samuel.

Is it possible to be unfaithful to someone who barely deigns to glance in your direction? The knights of old would have said yes, that constancy in the face of indifference is love in its purest form. Stendhal, on the other hand, would have written a letter explaining why that indifference would lead him to sleep with other people and if the woman he liked wanted to reach her full potential she should sleep with him whether she liked him or not. Stendhal had fallen in my opinion since reading the Penguin Great Loves edition of *Cures for Love*. What a creep. Chrétien de Troyes and his knights had it right, I think.

After two days the lake was noticeably closer, as were the great statues. It looked as if they were turning their heads to keep watching us. I hoped it was an optical illusion, of the kind that makes the eyes in creepy old paintings seem to follow you around the room, but I suspected it was not.

And then, disaster!

A gigantic crevasse snaked its way across the landscape. Nothing to those giants who had preceded us upon this route, it was to us as if the Grand Canyon had opened up before an ant. Though an ant, of course, would scarcely trouble itself with a second thought before working its way down one side of the canyon and then up the other, an option not available to we somewhat less agile biped mammals. We couldn't even see the bottom of it.

We sat down at its edge and nibbled on some bread. None of us spoke. There were no useful ideas to be had. No suggestions that might solve the problem. No way of getting across and no way of getting down. We were stuck, utterly stuck. The crevasse extended as far as we could see in either direction, so there was no getting around it. It had not been visible at a distance because this side was rather higher than the other, as if this continental shelf (if that is what these were, in this bizarre place) were crashing over the other, creating an illusion of continuity.

As we sat thinking, the most peculiar thing happened. A black disc appeared in the sky above the crevasse, then disappeared, then reappeared again off to our left side. It went again, then came back, and this time a cat – a cat, of all things! – peered out at us. The black disc disappeared again. Then popped up right above us, so close I could have jumped in had there been a trampoline to hand.

No cat, this time, but a girl. She poked her head out of the black disc – a hole, it now seemed – and stared at us with a curious smile.

Zeddy was the first to gather herself enough to speak. "Hello, young lady! Can you help us get across?"

The girl said nothing, but continued to smile, and four other holes popped up around us. In one I could see her left foot. In another her right arm. In another her queer little cat. And from the fourth emerged a man, an odd-looking man. He jumped down to the ground beside us and all the black discs disappeared, the girl and the cat along with them.

"Good morning," said the man with a flourish and an absolutely intentional smile. "You seem to be in the wrong place. Stranded, are you? Well, my name is Thornton Excelsior, and I think I can help."

V. The Voyagers Three

"Thanks!" I said, enthusiastically but without much optimism, to this strange chap who had popped up out of nowhere. "Who was your friend with the cat?"

"That was Helen," he replied. "Her cat is magic, poor girl, but she makes the best of it."

That stumped me for a minute, but Zeddy piped up with a question. "Couldn't she just have taken us across, with those magic portals of hers?"

Thornton Excelsior laughed gently, and then a little louder, as if testing its effect upon the weather. "No, it doesn't work like that. We both found ourselves here a few weeks ago, and we've been hanging out since then. The cat controls the portals, not Helen. The cat must have liked you. Or found you annoying and it wants you out of the way, there's no way of knowing. Not with cats. Now, we need a giant carrot."

"I don't think we have one," said Beatrice. "What do you want it for?"

"I'm happy to explain," said Thornton. "You need to cross this crevasse. Every crevasse contains an 'ass'. Donkeys like carrots. If we had a giant carrot we could get the ass to follow the carrot and pull the crevasse closed."

I stared at him with utter incomprehension. "That doesn't make the slightest bit of sense," I said, trying to be polite.

He laughed again. "Of course not, stupid me. Asses are far too stubborn for that to work! Let me think again."

Our initial excitement was fading, but at least he was more pleasant than staring at the statues, waiting for them to beam their death-rays at us once again.

"I have it!" he declared. "Give me a piece of your bread. Good, thanks! Now, the human neck contains as many bones as the neck of a giraffe, right?"

"I guess so," said Beatrice, reluctantly.

"Right, it does. But giraffes stretch all their bones out to make their necks longer. They have to, to reach their food, it's only logical! So I will throw your bread in the air, and you can stretch out your necks to their fullest length!"

"And how will that help us?" asked Zeddy.

"You'll be able to see further, which is helpful in any situation. Are you ready? Go!"

He threw the bread in the air. I have to admit that I did not really try to stretch my neck out further than its usual length. What would have happened to my throat if it had worked?

Thornton picked the bread up from the floor, looking somewhat crestfallen. "I'm sorry," he said. "That kind of thing normally works for me. It's as if... I don't know... things aren't quite right. As if I'm not being written by the right person."

"Don't give up," said Zeddy. She seemed quite sympathetic to him, much more so than she had ever been to Beatrice or me. "Some of us feel like that all the time. If you keep trying, I bet one of your ideas would work."

"Thank you for your empathy," he said with a slow smile. Then he had a new idea. I could tell, already, when that had happened. He virtually sizzled with energetic, vigorous thought. "Empathy! Reconciliation! Understanding!"

As each word left his mouth he took hold of it and laid it across the crevasse. And yes, I can't believe I'm writing that either. But it happened. I was there.

"Helpfulness! Friendship! Unselfishness!!" Each word was grabbed and added to the others. "It's working!" he said in an aside to us.

"What the hell is going on?" said Beatrice. "How is he doing that?"

"He's building bridges," said Zeddy. "I get it. Using bridge-building language to build a bridge. It makes perfect sense, when you think about it."

I gingerly placed one foot upon the bridge, even as Thornton continued to shout words. ("Reciprocity! Forgiveness! Apologies!") The first word seemed to hold my weight, so I tried another, and now I was standing over the crevasse.

I looked back to Beatrice and Zeddy. "I have the feeling that we shouldn't think about it too hard, we should just accept it and move on."

Beatrice was obviously reluctant, but Zeddy pushed her forward. We followed Thornton Excelsior across the bridge as he built it word by word, supplying him with bridge-building words of our own whenever he ran short ("Reasonableness!" "Honesty!" "Trust!"), and before we knew it we were all safely on the other side.

"We came a long way in that paragraph," said Thornton, and we all smiled as if we understood what he meant. He came to shake each of our hands – by which I mean grabbing us by the wrist and flopping our hands about – and we said our farewells. "You are where you ought to be now, aren't you? In the right place!" He looked me in the eye. "You're in the first person, Howard. You can do this."

And then he left the story.

From there it was almost a comfortable stroll down to the footprint-shaped lake. A river entered the lake on the left side of the heel and emerged by the little toe. The footstep of the stone god must have made enough of an impression for the river's waters to break and give birth to this new lake. I was beginning to grow nervous, it having now been almost three days since the stone gods last used their death-gaze. We needed to get out of their sight before it was unleashed once again. Luckily, life had flocked to the lake, as it tends to do, and a smattering of rickety jetties, wharfs, homes, shacks and huts had already been thrown up around its nearest bank. I hoped that we would be able to find transportation there of some kind, to help us cross the lake more quickly. We had been fortunate so far, but that could not last. Nothing does.

We had nothing to trade, which would usually have been a problem in a situation like this. Yet as we approached Lakeling (as we would later discover it to be called) we were welcomed enthusiastically by everyone. About half of the people there were Omnobisian, the other half human. It seemed that the lake had drawn many other new arrivals to its banks, and none of the other humans we talked to (over the hot broth eagerly pressed upon us) had any idea why they had been brought to this place. Few even thought that there was any reason to it. A pair of tank commanders called Marmite and Milo told me it was a military screw-up. If only they'd had their tank with them... A crew of spacers, working for now on a dinky little fishing boat they had christened the *Black Cygnet*, told us to make the best of it, get on with life. We asked if they would take us across the lake, but they shook their heads, albeit reluctantly. "Our ship wouldn't make it that far. Not yet."

We were on the point of giving up and setting off on foot when we heard a shout from above: "What ho!"

We had in the main been careful to keep out of the open, and when it could not be avoided we had dashed with our heads down and covered. It got us some funny looks, and maybe it was a complete waste of effort, but we were still alive. This was one of those occasions, so I had to uncover my head before seeing our interlocutor.

"Hello down there!" he called, from the oddest contraption I have ever seen: a small Georgian airship with a set of six bicycles beneath it, two of them occupied. One was our new friend, the other apparently his colleague. "We have just returned from mapping this here lake, and I hear you are looking for help in crossing it?"

He was William Broome, and his colleague Joseph Anstey, gentlemen map-makers from (they claimed) the eighteenth century, although it didn't sound like any eighteenth-century I had heard of. As we pedalled our way across the lake they told us stories of silver cities from the thirty-fifth century and worlds where giant oysters lived among endless desert storms and the spreading white void of Valiant Razalia and I don't know if I would have believed any of it if we hadn't been in such peculiar circumstances already. We were utterly grateful for their assistance, which must have taken days if not entire weeks off our journey. The far end of the lake was as far as they would be able to go ("The buoyancy only lasts so long, I'm afraid!") and that was good enough for me.

Beatrice seemed particularly happy with this mode of transportation. Her grin was so huge it must have brought puzzlement to my face. "I have something like this at home," she called across the wind, pedalling with all her might.

"Dash it, here's a rum thing!" shouted Anstey, whose bicycle was the one that controlled our course. He twisted his handlebars to the side, and called for us to pedal harder. "We need more speed, chaps!"

I gave it all I had, and looked around to see if I could spot the problem. Was it a storm? A flock of pterodactyls? Airship pirates? If only. The stone gods were looking our way, and their eyes were glowing bright red. Even at this distance it was almost blinding. And then came the blast. Incredible heat scorched my face, and in that moment I knew Anstey's quick thinking had saved us from death. That thought was still in the process of crossing my mind when a flume of superheated steam blew up from the lake below, doing its best to cook us like vegetables.

"Quite a pickle we're in," called Broome. "Time to turn again, I think, Jos."

"I couldn't agree more, Wm," responded Anstey, twisting the handlebars the other way, and I realised with horror that only one of the three stone gods had unleashed their death gaze.

The other two had still to fire!

VI. Stranded Educators

Space is limited, so we must hurtle through the rest of my story in the chapter that remains. Two more narrow escapes from the death-ray beams, thanks to the quick-wittedness of William and Joseph and the quick-footedness of Beatrice, brought us safely to the far bank of the lake, where we said goodbye to our new friends under the baleful gaze of the frustrated stone gods.

"Safe return," I said, rather earnestly.

"Thank you," said William. "It should be safe now those pests have exhausted their eyes."

Then they were gone, and we pressed on. We had plenty of food and drink, thanks to the generous people of Lakeling, so the only immediate problem was our fatigue, and that we pushed aside for a later day. A large hill, or perhaps you'd call it a small mountain, lay between us and our goal, and after two days of walking we climbed it like goats, working as a team and urging each other on. If I had once had my doubts about these two women, they were long gone now. They were forged of steel, and together we were unbreakable.

I could never have predicted what we would discover when we reached the top of that hill. There, at the feet of the stone gods, was a university. At least, that's what it looked like to me at first. But that was impossible. It just looked that way at a glance. It was a set of spacecraft, that had landed by the stone gods, in a pattern that to me recalled the layout of a university. But forget that: whatever they were, they could be the way out, for us, for everyone. I felt something stirring in my chest, something I had not felt for quite some time. It was, as you may well have guessed, hope. A not unwelcome feeling.

"Let's get down there," said Beatrice.

"Do you think they are controlling the stone gods?" asked Zeddy.

"I doubt it," said Beatrice. "Those things seem to know what they are doing. Just look at their faces. They don't look happy that they missed us."

It was true, they did not. Those faces, that had seemed so impassive the first time we saw them, now scowled and frowned in frustration, as if they were still reacting in slow motion to the airship's survival two days before.

"Look over there," said Beatrice, pointing to a place about a mile off to our left, where another small mountain left a way through to this valley of the statues.

It was difficult to see what was happening in any detail, but it looked like a small army – perhaps a hundred or so of them – was about to descend upon the valley. Apart from that, all I could make out was that the attackers were purple-skinned, unlike their pale leader, who wore a suit and sported a bushy grey beard. I looked at where they were heading, and saw another purple army – a half-naked one this time – rushing up to meet them from the area around the spaceships.

"It looks like the same split we saw back in Footprint and the woods," I said. "Those who worship the statues and those who are against them."

"Should we help the attackers?" wondered Beatrice.

"There's no time," said Zeddy. "The death-rays will be ready to fire again very soon, and the stone gods are still watching us. We should be glad those Omnobisians have left the statues unguarded and get down there while we can."

I couldn't help agreeing. This could be our only chance. (To do what? I still wasn't sure.) Beatrice was soon convinced, and we began to climb and then, once we could, jog down the mountainside, feeling now less like goats and more like goats' cheese, bumping along in a way that was not at all tasty. But we escaped the notice of the Omnobisians who had been hiding in the shadows of the stone gods only moments before, so we counted ourselves lucky. Very lucky.

As we approached the nearest of the spacecraft we saw frantic waves from one viewport, and headed in that direction. An airlock door swung open and we ran inside, not caring if it was a trap, just glad to be out of sight. Your priorities change when gods start trying to kill you with their eye-beams, believe me.

"Welcome to Space University Trent," came a male voice over an intercom, as the outer airlock door closed behind us. So my first impression had been correct! This was a university! A university that travelled in space to pursue its studies throughout the galaxy! Amazing! The voice continued: "I am Doctor David Lum, Professor of Philosophy. I hope we can be friendly, I assume that we will be, but I hope you will understand if I do not jump to conclusions given the situation we are in."

"Tell us more about the situation," said Beatrice. "Perhaps we can help." I nodded in agreement.

"I hope so," said Dr Lum. "Could you introduce yourselves, and tell us how you got here?"

I spoke first. "I am Howard, a writer. This is Beatrice, a police officer, and this is Zeddy, a musician. We all came to this place the same way: seeing a random image of the three statues in our everyday lives, then waking up in a giant footprint about nine days' walk away from here."

The inner airlock door opened, and in came a ruggedly handsome man in his early thirties. "Forgive Dr Lum, he has trust issues and can be somewhat fussy." A loud harrumph sounded over the intercom. "I am Mack Hardiman, special assistant to the vice chancellor. You've come a long way, and it's our fault. Let's get you to the canteen and we can talk while you fill up on fries. Does that sound good?"

It really did.

At the canteen we were joined by Laney Rashupon, Professor of Information, and Terry Leinster from the

Faculty of Medicine. All about us the usual business of a university seemed to be proceeding as normal.

"We've been stuck here for three years," said Rashupon. "We've had to get used to it."

"You can't get away?" asked Zeddy. "You have power."

"We've tried," said Leinster. "Every time we try to fly off one of the statues knocks us down again. There's no time to get off the ground. So we've got on with our studies. We're pretty self-contained. The Faculty of Agriculture provides food and water."

"Did you come here to study the statues?" I asked. "And what did you mean, you brought us here?"

The assembled university staff looked embarrassed.

"No," said Lum. "On this world there are the remnants of an ancient civilisation, destroyed in what seems to have been a cataclysm. Or it might have been a civilisation far in the future that was somehow memorialised in ancient times, it is hard to tell. We came to study the underground ruins in this valley."

Hardiman took up the story. "The History and Archaelogy departments had wanted to come here for decades, and they finally got their chance. But when they started to poke around, we realised that the ruins weren't actually all that ruined, and things started to happen."

"The planet started to spin at this ridiculously fast speed," said Rashupon. "Isolating us, making it almost impossible to escape even without the statues. And then the statues came. Somehow, they arrived out of nowhere—"

"Out of superspace, we think," interrupted Lum. "What some call the travelling dimension."

"Evidence is scant," resumed Rashupon, "but that's what we think. Then they walked over here, leaving those gigantic footprints everywhere, and settled in for a long stay. We think that getting here seriously depleted their power."

"Have you tried leaving?" asked Beatrice.

"Yes," said Hardiman, "and barely escaped with our lives. They shoot death-rays from their eyes. They've been using them a lot this last couple of weeks, so you have probably seen them."

"They were shooting them at us," said Zeddy with pride.

"And you survived?" Hardiman was clearly impressed. "We retreated here, and, soon after, local people began to show up, worshipping the statues and trying to force their way in. We were safe enough inside, but excursions outdoors were impossible unless we had been willing to defend ourselves to the death. Unconscionable when we are otherwise perfectly safe within. So we took another approach. You asked how we brought you here. I can show you. Have you had enough to eat yet?"

My third plate of chips was now empty, so I nodded, as did Beatrice and Zeddy.

"Then come with us, we'll show you."

As we followed him through the corridors of the university the stress under which these students, teachers and administrative staff lived was easy to see. Exhaustion showed on every face. Dr Lum explained that the three year stay on this world called Omnobis had given most of the students time to complete their undergraduate studies, and most had moved on to postgraduate work. Some had begun to start families. Even in such circumstances as that, life keeps trying. Or libido does. One of the two.

We arrived at the archaeology department, one of the most impressive things I have ever seen in a lifetime that has been rather amazing. Its focus was a huge hall with an open bottom – that's right, it was big enough to land upon a site of historical interest and actually do the dig inside the university! On our approach we received grim nods from students and faculty members who were noticeably cognisant of their responsibility for the current situation.

A metal walkway took us across the ground and then a small lift took us down into the earth. A short walk through a dank tunnel illuminated with temporary lighting brought us to a larger cavern. Beneath us was the main dig, students and their supervisors brushing away the dirt to reveal the mysteries hidden by time, but Hardiman pointed up. Most of the cavern's roof was rocky and dark, but there was one patch of bright white stone, from which emerged a tangle of probes and cables, leading to a bank of computers down below.

"The statue's heel," said Hardiman. "We hoped to tap into their power and send a distress call out from whatever they've done with this patch of space. But we underestimated that power. We didn't realise it would actually drag you here from your homes, summon you from worlds and times unknown."

"It isn't just us," said Beatrice. "We met others, too, lots of them, gathered at the lake, and others before that. You were more successful than you knew."

"And yet," said Dr Lum, "you were the first to make it this far."

"Not the first," said a gruff, rather pompous voice from the darkness. A man stepped forward, and I realised it was the man we had seen from a distance on the mountain, with a huge bushy beard and a roughed-up brown suit. "As ever, I, Professor Challenger, was the first to reach this long-lost place!"

VII. Wrath of the Stone Gods

"Professor Challenger! The great explorer!" I ran forward to shake his hand, though he was reluctant to hand it over. "It is a privilege to meet you."

"I'm sure it is," he said with a scowl. "And you, who are you and what do you do?"

"I am Howard Phillips, a writer."

He did not look happy. "Not a journalist, I hope?"

I shook my head. "A novelist, a poet, a reviewer, a songwriter, a short story writer, and a composer of jokes, but not as yet a journalist."

He nodded fiercely to indicate that this part of the conversation was over. He pointed at Hardiman. "You were explaining how you idiots brought us here to solve your god problem?"

"Yes," said Hardiman. "We were idiots. We are mere mortals, doomed to stumble on and on. How did you get here?"

"I was on my way to investigate reports of supernaturally possessed elephants in a remote part of India, reading a newspaper, came upon a photograph of your three statues, then found myself here. A village of locals were having trouble with their fellows, the chaps who were encamped around your space university, and I agreed to lead them in the assault."

"We saw," said Beatrice. "Very impressive. I think we would have died without your intervention. We had no idea a small army awaited us at the bottom of the mountain."

"The pleasure is all mine," Challenger said with his first genuine smile. "Now, what can we do to get ourselves home?"

Each of us stared at the others in silence for a few moments. Heroes, villains and holy fools, we should have had the answer between us. But the university staff had not anticipated that their rescuers would arrive without transport, without weapons, without anything that could possibly help in this situation – except our brains, our experience and our gumption, and we had plenty of that.

I began to feel like crying.

Suddenly we were bathed in daylight. The giant stone foot had been lifted, and the heel went with it. A baleful red eye glared down through the hole, and as we prepared to die, bathed in red heat, the eye was hidden by a descending hand, which broke through the cavern roof and scooped us all up into the air. Not everyone survived. I saw more than one student crushed beneath falling rock. Others escaped, scrambling away back down the tunnel before the hand lifted itself up. I focused on keeping my footing, and making sure I didn't fall into the gaps between the giant's fingers.

And then there we were, held at the height of the three giants' chests, three pairs of burning eyes staring, glaring, ready to burn us away like tissue paper in a fire. We were nothing to them, nothing.

But we were not dead yet. So I kept my tears back for now.

FOOLISH HUMANS. WHY TRY THE PATIENCE OF FINNITH?

It wasn't a voice so much as a knowledge that came to me with such force it was like a punch to the cerebral cortex. And I knew this voice came from the taller of the three statues, one who appeared male, with a hairless head. (Though of course the hair of the other two was of stone, as if carved, not true hair.)

FINNITH SPEAKS TRUTH. I, DALM, TIRE OF HUMANS TOO.

This was the stone god who presented as female. I felt her words in the pit of my stomach, churning at my guts as if I had swallowed a snake.

WE WERE A PEACEFUL CIVILISATION, TILL YOU CAME. AFTER ALL THIS TIME, WE RETURN HOME, ONLY TO BE VEXED BY YOU AGAIN. I, BRANT, WOULD SEE YOU ALL DESTROYED.

This was the other male statue, the one with hair carved upon his head, the one who held us in his hand. I noted with alarm that his fist was beginning to close upon us.

"We didn't mean to!" I shouted, forcing myself to break the spell of sheer shock that had kept us all silent till now. "We all just want to get home!"

HOME. I REMEMBER HOME, said Dalm. HAPPY WE WERE. OUR CHILDREN SANG IN CHOIRS. OUR ELDERS RELAXED IN THEIR ROCKING CHAIRS. OUR MEN AND WOMEN WORKED TILL THEY WERE DONE AND SLEPT SOUNDLY TILL MORNING. AND THEN CAME YOUR WEAPON.

"What weapon?" called Zeddy. "If we had a weapon that could hurt you, don't you think we'd have used it by now?"

YOUR NEWTON BRADDELL, said Finnith. WE WERE NOT LIKE THIS THEN. WE ARE THE SURVIVORS OF BRADDELL. HE CAME AS A FRIEND. THEN A STUMBLE, A TRIP, A SLIP AND A FUMBLE, AND OUR CIVILISATION WAS GONE, AS IF IT WERE NOTHING. WE THREE WERE ALL THAT REMAINED. EXPLORERS IN SUPERSPACE, WE RECEIVED A FINAL WARNING, NEWS OF THE UNFOLDING DISASTER, THEN NOTHING MORE. AND WE WERE LOST, TO CALCIFY AND GROW EVER LARGER IN SUPERSPACE.

UNTIL YOU SUMMONED US BACK, said Dalm.

"It was an accident," said Hardiman. "An accident!"

WE ARE NOT UNGRATEFUL, said Finnith. WE WERE LOST. NOW WE ARE NOT. BUT WE HAVE HAD ENOUGH OF THE HUMAN INFESTATION OF THIS WORLD. OF ANY WORLDS. WE HAVE SPUN THIS WORLD AND SOAKED UP THE STRENGTH OF EVERY STAR IN THE SKY. NOW WE WILL DESTROY ALL OF YOU, THEN DESTROY THE WORLDS YOU CAME FROM.

"Don't do it," cried Beatrice. "We are good people, mostly. Life isn't an infestation, it's a gift!"

The three stone gods laughed.

"We'll find a way to stop you!" yelled Professor Challenger. "I've dealt with your kind before. Death-hungry maniacs with more power than sense. And if we don't stop you, others will."

I'M SORRY, BUT NO YOU WON'T, said Brant. YOUR FRIEND TRIED TO USE MY POWER TO SUMMON HELP. IT GAVE ME GREAT PLEASURE TO ASSIST. I SUMMONED ALL THE HELP THERE COULD EVER HAVE BEEN, BROUGHT IT ALL TO THIS PLACE. TORN FROM SPACE AND TIME, STOLEN FROM FRIENDS AND HOME, JUST LIKE WE WERE BY YOUR BRADDELL, NONE OF YOU CAN DO A THING TO STOP US. ALL READY TO DIE AT ONCE, LEAVING THE UNIVERSE FREE TO LIVE WITHOUT YOUR BLUNDERING MALEVOLENCE.

Their six eyes glowed ever redder, and I think that would have been it for us, had Wm and Jos, the Voyagers Twain, not chosen that moment to fly down from the mountain in their ridiculous bicycle-driven airship. "Dash me, here's a thing!" said William, pedalling like the wind, as were the other four occupants of the craft: a pair of gents in matching jumpsuits, Bardello Fatloch, and little Taio, who had wooden blocks strapped to each foot so they could reach the pedals.

Down below, students, teachers and the remnants of Challenger's army emerged from the university's many faculties, attacking the feet of the statues with anything and everything that could make a dent in a hunk of rock: drills, maces, chisels, lasers and hammers, just to begin with, even high pressure hoses. Up above, the Voyagers Twain and their allies were dropping bags of wet flour and mud upon the eyes of the stone gods. None of it would have blocked their death-rays for a second, but I suspected that the stone gods still wanted to save power where they could – and were probably wary of blasting each other.

It would be mere moments before Brant thought to close his hand or shake us off like grains of sand, so we had to use those moments well. I thought back to the time I had spent living at the end of time with the Parang, the crystalline people of my bandmate J,J,T,L.M, who communicated with notes and chimes. I grabbed a piece of rubble from Brant's palm, and rapped upon his hand.

"Hear that note?" I asked Zeddy. "Can you sing it, three octaves higher?"

"I can try," she answered, and began to sing, a high-pitched note that was audible even above the noise of the pitched battle below and the angry roars of the stone gods.

"Everyone join in!" I shouted. "Sing the same note!"

As they all sang, getting as close to the note as they could, I laid my hand on Brant's palm, and felt the slightest of vibrations. It was slight, but it was enough for me to get in, back along the same psychic pathways he had used to bellow straight into our brains.

You pick up a lot when you have lived a life or two. BRANT, FIRE TO YOUR LEFT.

He followed the instruction, not realising it came from me. His death-ray gaze hit Dalm in the midriff, prompting her to unthinkingly unleash her own beams as she fell, and here we got lucky once again: she hit Finnish, and knocked him down to the ground.

END THIS MADNESS, I told Brant. TELL THE OTHERS TO LIE DOWN. YOU ALL NEED TO HAVE A LITTLE NAP AND THEN A NICE CUP OF TEA.

Thank goodness he listened, or I would have had to move on to my second idea. And that would have been more dangerous for us all.

Once Brant had laid down to sleep, we clambered down to the ground, where we were met by anxious university staff and students, and cheered by the Omnobisians. Soon we were joined by William and Joseph, Bordello Fatloch and Taio, and by their new friends, who called themselves the Two Husbands ("We found them swimming across the footprint lake," said William).

"Will you be able to do anything for them?" I asked Lum, Leinster, Rashupon and Hardiman. "I feel responsible, as a species."

"I think so," said Rashupon. "Now we know how they became this way, that it isn't natural, and they are no longer actively trying to kill us, I think we will be able to reverse what happened to them. We have the best superspace researchers in the galaxy here at Space University Trent. We won't be going anywhere till this world stops spinning so quickly and these poor people are back to normal."

"And serving time for all the people they murdered?" asked Beatrice, pointedly.

"It goes without saying," said Hardiman. "The Faculty of Law wouldn't have it any other way."

"And before you get them back to normal," said Husband Two, once he had introduced himself to us, "I think we can hook into their power to get us all home. I'll need..." He went on to list a hundred pieces of equipment, each of which was at his disposal before the day was out. He warned us before starting work that the process might leave us with only the vaguest memories of our adventures in this place, so I spent the day writing it all down in my moleskine.

As we prepared to go home, I sought out Beatrice and Zeddy. "Thank you for all your help and support," I said. "I think we might have saved the universe."

"No worries," said Zeddy with a jutting chin to show she didn't care. "It's been okay."

"It's been weird," said Beatrice. "But that seems to be my life nowadays."

And then I was back in Green Ties and Jam, wondering why I felt so tired.

Acknowledgments

The consequences of Newton Braddell's incompetence appear with the permission of John Greenwood. Braddell appeared in our magazine from issues 8 to 32.

Thornton Excelsior appears with the permission of Rhys Hughes. Thornton previously appeared in issues 38, 39 and 40. His complete adventures have now been collected in *The Lunar Tickle*.

Milo and Marmite appear with the permission of Ross Gresham. Their previous adventures can be found in issues 34, 41, 44, 46 and 49. Ross has a new thriller out soon: *White Shark*.

The crew of the *Black Swan* appear with the permission of Mitchell Edgeworth. They previously appeared in issues 40, 42, 43, 46, 47, 50 and 53.

The Voyagers Twain – William Broome and Joseph Anstey – appear with the permission of Michael Wyndham Thomas. More of their adventures can be seen in his novels *The Mercury Annual* and *Pilgrims at the White Horizon*.

Beatrice appears with the permission of Antonella Coriander, and previously appeared in issues 47, 48, 49, 50 and 51.

Professor Challenger appears without permission. You think he'd ask anyone before barging his way into a story? He previously appeared in issues one and two. The elephants he mentions are from Rafe McGregor's story "The Last Testament", in issue 37.

Zeddy Graves appears for the first time in this issue. But she will return!

Bardello Fatloch (also known as *The Fear Man*) and his daughter Taio first appeared in issues six and seven.

Howard Phillips gave himself permission to appear in this story. He has been a regular contributor to this magazine since issue four.

Helen and her magic cat were created by Steven Gilligan, and appeared in issues 12 to 22.

The staff of Space University Trent previously appeared in issue 13, while the Two Husbands appeared in issues 50, 51 and 52. Both appear with the kind permission of Walt Brunston.

Dodge Sidestep appears with the permission of Howard Watts, and previously appeared in issues 43, 50 and 53.

Howard Phillips typed up this novella after finding a draft version in his moleksine notebook. He does not remember writing it, and is not sure whether these events really happened or not.

My Place

Anthony Thomson

I first came across the name of Seabridge a short time after leaving the motorway and heading towards the south west coast.

One minute I was thinking about Marianne again, the next, I suddenly remembered that picturesque fishing port at the back of the little bay.

Like so many of the tourists who fought their way into the numerous gift shops lining that harbour, Seabridge barged into my thoughts, shouldering aside memories of my ex and parading itself up and down for show.

I remembered the pictures I'd seen of the place in the guides I'd skimmed through before leaving the city, all of them reeking of the archetypical coastal town and a magnet for tourists. Thankfully the place was miles east further down the coast and well away from the sleepy town of Rainswood where I was holing up in an attempt to escape my emotions.

A fruitless endeavour I'd soon seen through while seated at an empty services café some miles back.

And now here I was having my thoughts molested by the memory of a place I could have sworn I'd never visited before.

I drove down a winding lane hemmed in by tall hedgerows, clouds overhead skimming by as if pursued by some unseen prey. The surrounding fields and distant hills lay napping in the early afternoon sunshine.

I'd come back to this part of the country under the delusion it would pull me out of the fog of my ex-lovers leaving. I'd walked the coastal path as a student and a return to those more innocent times seemed a good idea.

Besides I'd been sulking too long.

I actually liked sulking; it tended to inspire me.

Any thought Marianne would try to get back with me had vanished when I heard she'd gone abroad without saying where.

We had argued before – usually when I sulked – and had always had a fiery relationship. The insults we'd hurled at one another in that last fight hadn't been cute though.

She walked out and so did I.

She'd gone abroad, so bollocks I was off to the coast.

I'd had a fairly successful career as an artist, but was growing more frustrated by my status, fed up with meeting people who said I was "the guy who played with things". Everyone said I supposedly "played" with buildings in my paintings; I supposedly "played" with faces, with geometries; the shape of the landscape was "twisted in a playful way".

Even if I'd painted a still life, people would try and spot what I'd been "playing" with.

I was heartily sick of that, and sulked about it so much that "spoilt little cretinous Christopher Pike", – Marianne's latest insult – was a little tired of his life.

Maybe that's why we broke up.

I pulled over onto into an old farm track and sat a while staring at the clouds – maybe I could "play" with those buggers over the next few days – and again played the scene of that final row in my head.

Then the memory of that bloody fishing port came barging in, only now I was inundated by the bland simplistic brochure speak that filled the pages of most guidebooks.

A crow gave a loud shriek of afternoon displeasure and took off. I reached over and took a can of beer from my bag, opened it and took a long drink.

Since leaving London all I had thought about was her. This was not what I had intended.

Get yourself back to what you do best. Think about you.

I needed a new project. This was going to be a defining moment in my life. The artist who "played" was going to change into the artist who "vandalised" things.

Somewhere farther along the coast, something stirred, and it wasn't at all picturesque.

I continued to the coast, surprised to find I remembered not only the tiny hamlets and fishing villages from my previous visit, but where to find the best views, the most spectacular walks, favoured attractions, tea rooms, guest houses and the most picturesque towns and villages. I suddenly remembered them all.

How I had come to know of the famous Postcard Library in Seabridge; the quality of scones in Mrs Perkins' tea rooms in that same town, let alone where to find the best pint of Foxcatchers in the county, I had no idea.

It was as if a guidebook had invaded my mind.

I was hopeless with guidebooks, skimming through the pages while collecting a few hastily forgotten names. If someone showed me a map I could become quite violent.

I might have wondered what was going on if the road not taken an alarming series of twists and turns and dived down into a shallow valley.

At the far end of this fishing port, Rainswood sat spread about a small bay.

I saluted it with a wave of the can, "Rainswood welcomes you. One public house 'The Hand'. One shop 'Deborah's'. One café, that'll be 'Deborah's' too."

I avoided the knot of narrow lanes and red slate roofed houses gathered about the little harbour, taking instead a rough track up onto the headland to the east. Here, a row of small cottages sat facing the sea.

I pulled in alongside the cottage at the end, got out and took in the long serrated arc of the west coast stretching out into the distance. Breaking cloud cover released shafts of iridescent sunlight to fall upon the waves.

"You would have loved it here," I thought, which helped no one, although the gulls crowing loudly overhead seemed to me to enjoy this fraction of suffering.

I was about to hurl the empty can at them when a tall mousy haired woman in an enormous grey sweater and jeans stepped out of the front door.

"Mr Pike?" She walked over and shook my hand. "Catherine Walker. The agent for the cottage, I've your keys."

I stared at her as though she was some crazy relative I'd been ignoring for an eternity.

"I've just finished sorting things out for you." She turned to gaze over the view and her smile lit my afternoon. "Everything to your liking?"

"Gobsmacked," I replied, and meant it.

While I was removing my things from the boot I saw her staring at me.

"Sorry," she laughed, "it's my husband, Andrew, he's a big fan of your work."

On cue my equipment tumbled out from the boot and she stepped over to help. The drive, guidebook in my head and memory of Marianne were all beginning to bite. "He loves your painting of the winged matchboxes swarming over the motorway, probably because he's seen so much of the thing."

I wasn't sure if she meant the motorway or the winged matchboxes.

She laughed again, "Thank goodness we have someone in Rainswood with a bit of imagination..."

Without changing her tone she took me inside to meet the cottage. After acquainting me with the complimentary plate of tea bags, pint of milk and packet of ginger biscuits in the kitchen, she said, "I suppose you'll find it very quiet round here."

Her smile deserted her as she added, "There are other places to visit of course, but that's for the tourists, as you're probably well aware of?"

"Pardon?"

"Seabridge," she said, "down the coast. That's where the tourists go."

The name teased my memory again.

I remembered the old church housing the Postcard Library and had a vision of the dark hulk of the Coach House Hotel rising above the town.

"No time for tourists. I'm here to work," I told her.

"That's good then," she said, returning to her former cheerful self.

I hauled out the barely read copy of the guidebook to the area, considerably heavier I felt than when I remembered packing the thing, and she gave me such a look, I thought I'd somehow insulted her. "They only tell you what they want you to see in those things," she said with bitterness, "it's all a pack of lies if you ask me... just someone else's opini—" She broke off, saying I was probably tired after the drive, mentioned the one store in town, wished me a comfortable stay and left before I could apologise for my guidebook.

The gulls were the first things I drew. But I turned them into monsters and gave them huge confused eyes, as if they were strangers to the world they inhabited. Then I took too many photos and sat down to send them to the few remaining friends I had back in the smoke.

It wasn't long before I became introduced to the almost nonexistent connections in that region. The instructions for the cottage said the place had a dial up connection if I wanted to use it, adding that, "it might seem a little slow".

I used the landline to call Tim, who only used a mobile, thus incurring a clout of a charge.

"You're all alone mate," he said, shouting into his phone as if making me out to be on the other side of the planet, "alone with that ridiculous mind of yours."

I thanked him and said I was missing Marianne.

He joked about that too, so I said I would phone him when he was feeling less happy.

I took a half hour to explore the village, then purchased an enormous amount of supplies from the store, returned to the cottage and made a pitiful meal, threw most of this away, sat upon the terrace and produced some equally pitiful sketches which I also threw away, grew frustrated with the beauty of the sunset, with the gulls and the distant waves, and at myself and Marianne for the same reasons.

Finally I let my gaze settle on the settlements of lights appearing on the wide curve of the bay and sat and sulked.

Rainswood's only pub, *The Haven* was a small, quiet, unpretentious place with a torturously low ceiling, dark oak panelling that sucked the light from the corners and a large redundant fireplace flanked by two models of sitting cocker spaniels, smoking pipes. There was a small public bar with bare white walls and two tables and a much larger saloon; the walls of which were cursed with anaemic paintings of the coastline. I took a stool in the latter and sulked through a beer.

A couple of large windows offered views of the harbour, but each time I turned to gaze across the room I came under the scrutiny of those at the tables, all of whom seemed to have some interest in my being there.

At first I smiled. I always do in unknown places. As this seemed to scare the woman and anger the men I tried to look as stone faced as possible. This I found quite easy, my second drink bringing a resolution to forget Marianne, my past life, and remain there, stuck to the stool at the bar surrounded by dismal landscapes and glowering expressions and a harbour sick with shadows.

"Mr Pike I presume?"

I took a moment to revive my interest in the present and found a broad robust figure in a huge blue sweater grinning at me.

His smile, dressed within the grip of a thick black beard, took me by surprise, as did the murmur of conversation and occasional laughter around the bar, which had by then become quite full.

"I'm Andrew Winters. My wife met you earlier, at the cottage? I take it you are Mr Pike? Everyone else in here is familiar so I figured you must be our new guest."

He looked away to the barman who laughed and said, "No one else here I ain't seen before."

I found my manners after a moment and we shook hands and he offered me a drink saying, "I'm a big fan," which received an odd look from a little man in dirty overalls beside him.

"This man is a well known painter, Bernard." Mr Winter told him.

Bernard forced a smile before taking his drink back to his table.

Andrew asked how I was settling in and we exchanged banal pleasantries a while.

"I teach geography to those who want to listen at the college in the big place, some twenty five miles west," he told me. "We moved here to 'get away' and bring the kids up by the sea some years ago. Chris manages the letting agency. I'm the only one here who works outside the village, isn't that right Tony?" A giant of a man with a long morose face stared at us as if we were fools and nodded.

I had always been wary of tall people. They always seemed to me to be looking out on a different world.

"You say so, Mr Winters," this one said, loping away to join his fellow locals in the corner.

I hadn't been expecting to meet someone like Andrew Winters in a place like this. It was a pleasant surprise to find myself in a conversation about artists, and more to the point, my work.

I could tell by his enthusiasm that this amused and enthusiastic teacher was a little bored within his "quiet" community and hoped his job gave him enough interest. I would have probably gone crazy. Maybe he had. He laughed and spoke louder than anyone there as well as seeming to know everyone as though they were a relative. Judging by the looks he got this was obviously not the case.

While we were talking I'd begun to notice that the small crowd around the corner table were watching us with some amusement. I wasn't quite sure what was going on, but money seemed to be changing hands.

Andrew stopped smiling.

"Local custom," he said following my gaze, "just play along with it."

I was still wondering what he meant when the giant with the mournful face returned to the bar and stared down at me.

"You here to explore then?" he asked.

I looked up into his long weathered face, detecting a hint of amusement in his gaze.

"He's a painter, Tony," Andrew said, irritated, "a well known one at that."

"So you going to paint our village then?"

I stared at him, "I might. I might not."

If he had asked if I was going to "play" with the landscape I would have gone ballistic. I was in that sort of a mood.

Andrew put his hand on my arm, whispering, "Local custom, forget it."

The giant ignored this and glanced over to the corner where a stout figure with cropped ginger hair took out a stopwatch.

I was aware of the barman and others in the pub staring at me.

"What about Seabridge then? You going to paint over there?"

I was about to ask what business it was of his what I painted when I felt a tug at my memory.

As if chuffed to have been given an invite, the images of the fishing port along the coast rushed back.

The little harbour town at the back of the wide bay with the steep winding streets, flights of steps everywhere and the tall harbour walls with the narrow houses on top and the formidable bulk of the Coach House Hotel overlooking it all.

The giant watched me closely, then looked at his watch and shouted, "Forty five seconds," to those in the corner.

The figure at the table checked the stopwatch and nodded, "Forty five it is."

Someone gave a shout and the group began passing round notes and coins.

Tony patted me on the back, saying, "thanks for that matey," and wandered back to his mates.

Andrew stared after him, "Forget it."

Being ambushed by memories of a coastal town I'd never visited wasn't something I felt I could forget.

"Look, it's just a game Chris," he said in a lighter tone, "the locals are only too pleased to palm any visitors along the coast to that place. It keeps their little village trouble free. Mind you some nights The Hand could do with the trade, eh Jonas?"

The barman shook his head. "Could and couldn't."

The noise in the corner soon quietened down and a more convivial atmosphere returned.

"I'd advise against a visit," Andrew said later. "There's nothing there you won't find in a guidebook or on a postcard."

I felt that covered just about every picturesque little fishing village on the west coast.

Even though he laughed at this, I could see the unease in his expression, and the barman continued to give me the odd curious stare.

I decided to return to our previous conversation and ordered another round.

Before we parted Andrew returned to the subject of Seabridge, insisting it wasn't worth a visit.

"Leave the tourist traps to catch the unwary, Chris," he said, "I've a small boat I use for exploring those secluded bays you want to see. Once the weekend's here I'll treat you."

I said I'd take him up on the offer and walked back to the cottage.

A clear sky and full moon illuminated both sea and cliffs. There were stars everywhere.

I soon forgot the "local customs".

Seabridge, though, was now firmly embedded in my memory.

The next morning I gathered my equipment, took an all too brief look at a map of the area and set off to explore.

I had decided on the westerly arc of the coast, a wild uneven area of steep cliffs, sinister inlets, and menacing pinnacles of razor sharp rock rising from the troubled surf.

This soon proved to be less accessible than I'd thought. The headland was exposed to the fierce winds coming over the cliffs and the terrain rose and fell as if the land were imitating the waves below.

I managed some brief sketches while hiding behind some tormented bushes and crawled on my belly to the cliff edge to take photos of whatever secluded bays lay imprisoned down there.

In the end I gave up and trudged wearily back to the village where I helped the local economy by buying a bun and mug of coffee in the solitary cafe and returned to the cottage.

Once uploaded onto my laptop I looked through the photos I'd taken and attempted to work on the best of these (which amounted to half a dozen, most of them blurred), then on a whim plugged into the net and waited an age for a connection to stir.

I typed in Seabridge.

(This took another century to load, during which time I was confronted with a white screen and the image of a grinning seagull winking from the top right corner.)

The site was massive.

Apart from a vast compendium of stuff on all the

major sites of interest, there were links to not just the most popular areas but, as far as I could tell, every single street in the place, and from there links to even more detailed sites covering the more intricate histories of those streets.

My attention span for such things being almost zero, I zipped through an article about the legendary Postcard Library and switched off.

For such a small town, Seabridge seemed to have a lot going for it.

The next day I set out east and discovered the terrain (although still demanding) to be a far more attractive prospect.

Amongst the giant boulders, gritty dunes and slicks of dark serrated rock I found small secluded bays where even the shrill cries of my constant companions could not take away the pleasure.

"Dreams walk here!" I shouted at the gulls, and delighted, spent the day meandering around trying to find them.

The following day I set out to walk farther down the coast.

It was an untidy morning, clear, but with a nagging wind and fleeting clouds, and I'd drunk too much wine the night before, and at some late hour sent Marianne a text. Stupid. Stupid. Stupid.

So I meandered down the coast, exchanging pleasantries with the gulls and wondering why I'd broken a cardinal rule.

She hadn't returned my self pitying message.

Who would?

I had just sketched a group of miserable looking boulders I thought I could "play" with, and was about

to yell at the gulls again, when I realised they'd
disappeared.

Turning round I saw them bickering at the surf far
back in the distance.

For the first time all morning all I could hear was
the waves and the wind.

A short distance away a long tongue of rock and
wild grasses jutted out into the sea. I followed the path
around this and found myself staring out across the
blue waters of a wide bay to where a small town sat
spread out over a low hill.

Just as in all the photos I'd seen. there was the long
harbour and quay with its tawdry cascade of gift shops,
galleries and tea houses; the jetties bright with
decorated fishing boats; the seemingly endless warren
of rising winding streets; the narrow white and pink
houses above the tall stained sea wall; the endless
flights of steps linking the narrow streets; and atop it
all, the dark and imposing edifice of the Coach House
Hotel.

"Welcome to Seabridge," I said, although there were
no gulls to answer me back.

I stood a moment watching the crowds, most of
them taking photos as they made their way amongst
the converted warehouses along the harbour; a busy
hum of excited voices reaching me like some carefully
chanted hymn to the glories of cheap souvenir shops
and cosy tea rooms.

A small way on the path was cut off by an enormous
car park; row upon row of empty vehicles basking in
the midday sun.

I looked around but couldn't see a soul. Everyone
appeared to be either in the town or on the crowded
quayside.

I navigated a path around the cars and made my
way to the entrance and a road that kept to the
contour of the long hilly ridge that flanked the west of

the town. The road was empty but for a line of enormous coaches, parked one behind the other with their drivers sleeping on the front seats.

In contrast to the busy harbour front, the heavy silence emanating from these parked behemoths was disquieting.

I stepped between two of the coaches to gaze at the wedge of dark woodland occupying the opposite shore.

Below me the crowds pushed and shoved their way into and out of the cavernous gift shops that had been created out of old warehouses. They reminded me of a swarm of bees in a hive. Almost everyone I saw was busy either photographing the harbour and shops without any care for what they were seeing. No one was looking at the quiet blue water of the bay, or the brightly decorated fishing boats parked along the jetties.

A reckless current seemed to drive them on, from one shop or tea room to the next, pulling them from the packed quayside around and out into the narrow surrounding streets where they pushed and shoved their way to photograph the ancient shops or deliver them of their horde of tacky souvenirs.

It was so overpowering, I almost felt like joining them.

I whipped out my pad and hastily sketched this sightless mass, overjoyed to have something to lighten my mood.

Trying to latch onto individual figures was difficult though as they kept disappearing into the melee.

It made me weary just watching them.

I noticed some of the houses and shops had the figure of a fat orange man built just below the roofs, giving the impression they were bursting forth from the walls.

I counted eight different faces, each stamped with

the same malicious smile, and each naked but for a slip of red loincloth about their privates.

While I studied these aggressive overweight orange cherubs, I felt a sudden impulse from the unending mass of tourist fuelled havoc below.

The curious murmuring created from their incessant exchanges began to infiltrate my senses and I perceived that they were having more than excitable conversations.

Whatever they were saying, they were repeating themselves.

I stepped back through the passage between the coaches and walked farther down the road, eventually finding a flight of steps that would take me into a quieter, less troubling area of the town.

Those few souls that had found themselves likewise in these swiftly ascending back streets seemed no less feverish in their attempts to capture the narrow houses squeezed there, or indeed the gift shops that still prevailed between the cramped curtained windows like some bad rash.

I stopped and began to sketch one of the figurines supposedly exploding from the wall of one of the houses.

"Interesting isn't he?" a high nasally voice said beside me. "Probably thirteenth century. That's when the sea was worshipped you know. Not this sea. The forgotten sea. I've actually come across writings that say people believed water to speak..."

I turned to find a tall gangly looking man of some middle years staring at me in a surprised manner.

"The orange man," he said, pointing at the roof, "he arose from the ether and made of the air the world he wished to imagine. It's a fascinating legend. I've spent so long on it I think it's devoured me." He chuckled to himself and added, "Sand by the way. Jeremiah Sand."

I stared at his hand and then back at him.

He was absurdly pale, had a thin narrow face with reddened eyes, a thatch of straw colour hair, oddly pointed chin and wore a long shabby frock coat of the type Quakers once wore. His huge brown sandals, I saw, were covered in mud.

"They're quite strange," I said, declining his hand.

"You've been drawing them I see," he said, staring at the sketch I'd just completed.

"I've never heard of any orange man," I told him.

"Oh, it's very obscure, very obscure," he said in a deeper voice, and smiled, "very obscure."

I saw he owned just the two expressions; amusement or its twin, and wondered if he had some mental switch on the back of his neck for either.

"It appears to be a popular town," I said, feeling mildly uncomfortable because he was staring at the ground as if it had just insulted him.

"It is, it is, but the visitors get so carried away. I suppose one gets drawn into it... if you don't mind the pun. I take it you are also from along the coast?"

I told him about Rainswood and the cottage. He seemed to find it all rather surprising.

"Well that sounds... like some incredible dream, Mr?"

I revealed my name, he repeated it as though it were a piece of stray poetry he'd found in the street.

"Well, Mr Pike, we must follow our follies mustn't we? Mine I am afraid is this place and its ridiculous mystery. I'm a scholar of sorts you see, a scholar of my own obsessions, this place being one of them. Now the orange man..."

He seemed to gather all the frailty and oddness about him and become more solid; introducing me to a history of the figures bursting through so many of the walls of the houses of the town and explaining various snippets of Seabridge's long and convoluted history, most of which I didn't hear because I was trying to memorise his appearance. Apparently he had written a number of books on the place, none of which I had the remotest knowledge of.

He asked if I would join him for a cup of tea.

Knowing I could use him in a future work, I accepted.

We walked through the warren of those less crowded streets, up and down numerous flights of steps until finally arriving at a rather quaint tea shop nestled above the sea walls. It seemed to me the journey should have been shorter than it actually was, although the way Mr Sand walked, in a jerky almost undecided way, I suppose this made perfect sense.

Mrs Perkins' Pots and Postcards was a stuffy circular room with bow windows looking down onto the frenzy of the harbour. Most of the customers at the tables looked exhausted. Through an awning at the back I saw other rooms and a quiet clatter of cutlery and chink of china seemed to permeate the air like the buzzing of tiny insistent insects.

A small portly lady smelling of cheap talc came over, addressed Mr Sand loudly and took our orders.

"Will you be needing one?" she asked, and I saw she was about to lay some postcards with views of the town before us.

"Oh no, no, no, no. Not today Mrs Perkins," Mr Sand, replied.

His conversation throughout the walk there, and now that we were sitting down, seemed to alternate between one with himself and one with myself.

And there was something about his face that irritated me.

"You know they seek something that is never there." I saw he was staring at me. "You do understand that do you?"

"What do you mean?"

"It's an illness, all this 'seeing'. There really is

nothing there to see, if you see what I mean." He gestured down to the harbour. "I think they are all seeing something that isn't there. By the way the scones here are beyond delicious, quite out of this world."

He then switched to talking about the orange man again.

I turned to observe those around me.

It was the first time in that odd little town I'd experienced people who were actually motionless, although I saw this was not necessarily the case.

All the customers in that stuffy over-decorated room were looking at postcards.

One man, a tall figure in a tweed jacket with a blue-handled walking stick leant against his table, held a pair of postcards in either hand and kept staring from one to the other as if his life depended upon it.

Two elderly women in the far corner were contemplating their own cards in silence, turning them over to read the back and then returning to the picture on the front as if reading a book.

Our tea arrived in a large pot which Mrs Perkins had difficulty relaying to the centre of our table.

Mr Sand seemed delighted and bit into his scone with gusto.

"A teapot to rule the world with eh Mrs P?" he joked.

"It's a size," she said chuckling, "but we know how much you love your tea and scones."

"Size," he said loudly and gave a deep sigh, "size traps us all Mrs Perkins, size traps us all..." and lost his smile.

I found him an exhausting companion; alternating between the frivolous and the arcane before waffling off into something resembling his own troubled brand of existentialism.

I drank three cups of tea, failed to finish the scone he had ordered for me and said I had to go.

He merely smiled and said yes repeatedly. I went to pay but he shooed me off saying, "Next time," with some assurance. I stood up to leave and saw through the opened doorway at the back of the room not one, but five or six adjoining rooms, each with the customers at their tables staring intently at postcards.

I chose to walk along the street above the sea walls away from the chaos of the harbour.

As I did so, I couldn't shake off the feeling that Mr Sand was sitting there, by the bay window, watching me, even though the tea rooms were lost to view.

The postcards had probably been borrowed from the Postcard Library I remembered reading about. Maybe it was a custom around those parts.

It was only later, as I was hurrying back along the coastal path, I realised how absurd that sounded.

On my way to find the steps that would take me up onto the road, I came across a small shuttered shop with an excessive amount of guidebooks in the window and Seabridge Books written on a sign above the door.

Curious, I stepped inside.

From within a forest of tall postcard stands a large bearded figure glanced up at me.

I asked if he had any books about the town.

He stared at me a long moment before giving a shrug towards the bookcases on the far side of the room.

After a quick browse of the shelves I realised the entire wall was filled with Guides to Seabridge, as well as numerous maps of the town laid out on a table.

I glanced through a few of the books, surprised by

the amount of information available inside. The texts were uniformly bland, the photos too bright.

Each of those I glanced through contained a chapter entitled "What To See" and seemed to be a mistaken attempt at wry humour.

A door in the corner led into another smaller room, also filled with books.

There were more guides in here, as well as histories of the town and a number of biographies of famous local personalities, all of whom I'd never heard of.

And there were more maps laid out upon more tables.

It took a moment to realise, though, that these were guides not just to the town, but to each of the various areas. Some shelves were crammed with guides to the Harbour area, others with guides to the Coach House Region or the Postcard Quadrant.

There was an awful lot of detail about areas I could only surmise comprised of four or five streets.

Upon unfolding a map I peered a long time at the intricate detail presented.

To the side of the room another doorway led into a smaller room, and this was also filled with books.

Again the shelves were filled with guidebooks and again there were maps laid out across the tables.

After studying the titles I saw the guides now centred upon the town's individual streets. Naturally the promenade along the harbour front took precedence; there were five shelves packed with guides covering everything from in depth descriptions of gift shops, and their layouts, to complex diagrams of tea rooms.

The wealth of information was breathtaking.

I skimmed through a volume concerning Skittle Street, and another detailing the glories of Fandle Lane, where a mere hundred pages detailed the delights of the Postcard Library.

In the corner I discovered another door leading into a yet more cramped room. I stooped down and entered, finding once again all the walls filled with guides; these I soon saw, contained vast repositories of information about individual houses of the town, as well as a wealth of bland but colourful photographs.

The same intense script informed me in minute detail of what was to be found in, say, No 87 Sheffway Street. I read about the upstairs bathroom at No 81 Blown Street, with the bonus of a small map to accompany this.

There were at least four to six guides to every house in the town.

And in each, as with those of the first guides I had seen, there were sections titled, "What To Look Out For", where the text diverted from the banal to something almost arcane.

It was within this small room I wondered at the absence of any sound, and a feeling that I was somehow being watched, although there were no other customers there or any windows, just another doorway leading into a still smaller room, also filled with books.

I suddenly felt as if the front of the shop was somewhere far away and that I had been strolling through these rooms for an age.

A pair of steps led me down into the next room. I studied the guides and stepped back a little concerned. No longer to do with any landmarks or buildings, they were guides to certain individuals who lived in each of the houses and shops of the town. Or so I presumed, before coming across shelf upon shelf entitled, "Visitors".

Amongst yet another raft of histories and biographies I found a huge book entitled *An Encyclopaedia of Seconds in the Life Of*, and another filled with black and white photographs detailing the life of *The Blind Servant of Coach House Lane*.

There were maps on the tables. I did not bother with these, such was my surprise to find yet another door leading down into yet another room.

I glanced through at the books on the shelves and stepped back in surprise.

Then I left, trying as calmly as possible to make my way back through the rooms and not a little worried by the possibility that I could become lost in there.

As I hurried through the room whose guides more reasonably described just the regions of the town I saw a shelf containing some short volumes by one Jeramiah Sand.

Most covered the town's various legends and myths, others the curiously involved history of the place and one appeared to be a bizarre volume dedicated to scones.

On the back cover of each was a photograph of the scholar sitting at a table in Mrs Perkins' Tea Rooms looking unamused. A short brief underneath stated, "Jeramiah Sand is Seabridge's eminent historian and observer of town life. Without him our past would be lost."

I returned to the front of the shop feeling as if I'd been on a long journey to a place I would never truly remember and that it had been fraught with dangers.

I picked up a "Small But Significant Guide to Seabridge", and took it to the counter.

"You'll enjoy that," the burly figure said, staring up from the postcard he was studying. "It's a book."

When he didn't laugh I did it for him and stepped back outside.

I glanced through "A Small But Significant..."

There was a small map inside. It covered all the streets and main thoroughfares of the town.

It was not all that long. It didn't need to be.

I looked back and wondered if maybe there was a guide and map to Seabridge Books.

The drivers of the coaches were still asleep, each snoring peacefully at the front of their vehicles.

I stood awhile watching the scene on the quayside.

Something about that great river of tourists snapping their cameras and dashing in and out of the endless gift shops unsettled me.

Rather than bees, I was more inclined to think of those great shadows filled with starlings one sees in the autumnal skies.

I looked up to the maze of winding streets and stairways rising above the harbour and my glance fell upon the row of small houses huddled above the tall sea wall.

No doubt Mr Sand was still up there, perched at the window and scoffing his scone while ruminating over the orange man and seemingly tormented by the demands of size.

Then I left, hurrying down the road, through the packed car park and back onto the coastal path and the quiet sanctuary of empty coves and secluded beaches.

When I returned to the cottage I set about drawing scenes from the town, cursing that unlike those obsessed spectators, I had not thought to take any photos.

But while I remembered Seabridge quite clearly, whatever images came to mind seemed to have been transposed from the guidebooks. I soon found the reality of the place playing havoc with my memory.

The crowds for instance, I saw as one body, as if all their individual faces had been smeared to a blur. For some reason I was under the impression a lot of them had been wearing sunglasses.

The floor was soon littered with rushed sketches as I sought to remember details.

Seabridge Books became problematic. I couldn't be sure I had been alone in those small rooms.

It was as if my memory had been on a walk with a stranger.

Mr Sand I remembered through his only two expressions.

The figure in the tea rooms with the blue handled walking stick, I was pleased to have captured. The poor sod looking as if he was going quietly mad, continuously switching between those two postcards.

I saw now that all those giant boulders and bays I had originally come to paint had been made redundant.

I had found my project.

"Sounds like any other little tourist trap to me," Tim said when I called him. "Most of those people probably only ever get to see where they've been by looking at the photos they were taking all the time they were there. I'd leave well alone and go swimming or look for mermaids if I were you, Chris. You can find places like this anywhere."

"I've already done mermaids," I said, "remember?"

Marianne had posed for those. I could see her now dressed in a red and gold number stretched out on the top of a double decker bus I'd spent an age to persuade her to pose on.

"Well go swimming with the dolphins then. This

place sounds like some sort of Tourist Park for the unstable."

I didn't expect him to understand and rang off.

For the rest of that evening he texted "mermaids" to me every half hour and I replied with as much venom as I could muster.

I would have sulked but the excitement of that odd tourist nightmare filled me with inspiration.

I stayed up late working on some of the drawings, struggling to fill in the details, the expressions on the faces in the crowds, the miserable figure in the bookshop, that portly orange figure bursting through the walls, the hotel that always seemed to have its lights on even with the sun shining overhead.

For some reason the scale of the place eluded me. Were the fishing boats tiny?

How long was the harbour front?

How big was the hotel in relation to those narrow cottages?

Why had the gifts shops seemed so cavernous inside?

Was I going crazy?

The following morning I awoke around dawn and wandered out onto the terrace.

The sight of the sun rising over the sea and the mirage infested coastline was overwhelming.

I sat there a long time while the gulls flew by and screamed at me.

For some reason the events of the previous afternoon seemed far away, as if dreamed them up. Even the sketches I'd drawn seemed to have emerged from my imagination rather than a real place.

That evening I visited the Hand, where I met up with Andrew Winter and his wife.

Apart from the odd curious glance and obscure remark, the night passed without any weirdness.

I didn't mention where I'd been to Andrew, although I thought he was watching me closely throughout the evening. Chris seemed cheerful enough though so I avoided any mention of guidebooks, or that place along the coast everyone seemed so intolerant of.

The next morning I packed my equipment, plus two cameras, and set off along the coast.

As I approached that tongue of rocky headland, I again became aware of the cries of the gulls drifting away behind me. Once again I followed the path into the bay and stopped by the edge of the car park.

A low grassy slope led down to the water. I stood here a time and took photos of the town stretched out across the hill; of the tall green-stained sea wall and ominous black and grey hulk of the hotel overlooking it all.

Then I turned to the car park.

It was full again, and a number of coaches were lined up along the road.

I looked down at the water lapping the grassy bank, across to the trees on the opposite shore, and back to the car park.

I climbed over the low wall and made my way around the cars to the entrance. The owners were all in the town, just as they had been on my last visit.

I stopped to look at one or two vehicles.

The smell of warm pastry wafted over from the quay. I could hear the murmur of excited voices, and remembered what I'd heard upon the last visit.

I walked up alongside the giant coaches and stared up at the drivers asleep in their seats.

The frenzied crowds were again thronging the quayside, the busy murmur of excited voices permeating the air. This time I took dozens of shots, focusing in on the animated faces; on the busy gift shops; the pushing and shoving going on; the current of human bodies pressing and pushing one another into those narrow streets.

Then I stopped and walked back to the car park and took half a dozen photos of the cars and the coaches.

Then I photographed the road and stood a short time staring along it.

In the end I decided to postpone going into Seabridge and instead walked along the road, following it as it ran alongside the town and climbed up over the hill.

Here I found myself staring out across an expanse of dank brown scrubland.

After a quarter of a mile of stretching out along this barren headland the road stopped.

There was no tailing off. It just stopped.

One minute there was a straight edge of asphalt and then an earth track led out across some fields. Some distance away I could just make out the ribbon of motorway I'd turned off from some days before.

I took a lot of photographs of the end of the road, then turned around and walked back.

The sight of the sea and the coastline from the top of the hill felt comforting, as if the world outside the bay existed in a more sensible place.

I stopped a short way down and took photographs of the warren of tiny streets and the numerous flights of stairs.

By now I'd gone from feeling fairly pleased with the world to one of extreme irritation with anything to do with Seabridge.

I stared over the little fishing port tumbling down around the bay as if it had insulted me.

Even if a separate and unseen road had run along through the trees on the other shore, there was no way the streets were wide enough for that amount of traffic to pass through the town.

I followed the road back down to where it ran alongside the busy harbour and returned to photographing the crowds.

Something about the way they moved through the tiny streets seemed to be premeditated. Maybe they weren't behaving like starlings. Maybe they were behaving like ants, and were collecting for the nest.

This close, I could even feel the manic attraction of that feverish mass.

It was as if for a moment all the noise of their busy pushing to and fro and incessant murmuring vanished and a heavy silence hung over the whole scene.

I glanced up to the hotel.

It seemed to absorb the light in the surrounding streets and cast shadows over the area it dominated.

Curiosity got the better of me then and I descended the harbour steps and stood on the edge of the crowd as it rushed by.

The speed and fury of their movement was surprising, reminding me of those insane bull runs that take place in Pamplona in Spain. I tried to take some photos but lost my balance. People were suddenly pushing by me, taking pictures of the shops and the houses, rushing this way and that, affecting to be interested in all they saw, but with sudden flashes of sheer terror crossing their faces. I tried to step back but was overwhelmed by a current of majestic confusion.

In my panic I struck out and hit someone with my camera. The victim, a dark haired figure in a short sleeved shirt, paused to take my photo then carried on by.

I kicked out pushing back a woman in a bright red

dress and sun hat who smiled at me, before taking my photo.

As she turned to disappear back into the crowd I heard her saying, "The scenery is fabulous. We're staying in a lovely hotel and the breakfasts are very good. Marjorie likes the shrimp. See you soon, love Joan."

As the crowd swallowed her I heard her repeating the message.

"We're having such a lovely time. Yesterday we visited the museum and ate pastry on the quay. Very exciting."

I stared at the portly figure struggling through the crowd shouting out this message.

And then I thought I could hear the whole frenetic mass of them, all chattering away with their endless cycle of bland messages.

Just the sort of thing people scribbled on the backs of postcards.

I regained the steps and climbed back up to the road.

By now I wanted to run away through that vast car park and get back to the sea.

But the current of that other sea below pulled me back into the town.

I resisted enough to get away into the warren of narrow lanes.

It was there, wandering around as if I had been at sea for too long, I came across the Postcard Library.

It looked familiar because I'd seen it in the Guidebooks and on the website.

An old shrunken church with tall arched doors, a gaudy sign and posters either side advertising coming exhibitions.

I stepped inside, picking up on the musty smell of old carpets and lost incense. A small stone hallway opened onto a series of long white rooms filled either side with bookcases, their shelves crammed with postcards. Overhead the tall slanting ceiling's pair of enormous windows flooded the room with sunlight.

The atmosphere was quiet and calm. I watched people taking handfuls of cards to the tables where they sat studying each one intently.

At the far end of the room a pair of doors opened onto another similar room; aisle upon aisle of shelves crammed with postcards and sunlight spilling through the overhead windows.

Above the doors hung a huge image taken from a postcard of the scene down at the harbour.

Blown up to such extraordinary proportions, the crowds massed about the quay seemed transformed into something far more menacing. Their expressions were twisted, the cameras covering so many faces like newly transmuted eyes stared down into the library. Even the souvenirs they paraded so proudly were like some new form of weapon.

Anywhere else and I might have admired such a horror, but not in Seabridge.

I was about to take my own photograph of the thing – thus becoming a part of the symmetry of that confused town – when a voice said, "Seabridge Library is a font of all understanding. Can I help?"

I turned to find a mousy looking woman staring at me as if I'd just ruined her idea of the good life.

"Pardon?"

"Seabridge Library does not welcome cameras," she said, "what moment can I help you with?"

I stared at her, feeling the telescopic eyes of those giant figures on the wall peering down at us.

"Moments?"

"This room contains yesterday's moments," she said brightly. "The room beyond that contains moments from the day before, and the room farther on, the day before that. All moments are arranged in alphabetical order. You may enjoy a seat at one of the tables to digest your moments."

She seemed amiable enough so I asked how far back the "moments" went.

"Five years," she said smiling. "Which day do you think you will need?"

I stared through the doors into the other room and saw, in the distance, doors leading through to another room. No doubt it went on quite a way.

"The original day," I said, remembering a series of "playful" paintings I'd done some years before; "a waste of blasphemy" according to my least favourite critic.

"That's too far away," she said with a worried look, "you could only go there with the assistance of a Librarian."

"Fine," I said, surprised by there being such a room. "Librarian?"

"I would advise against it."

I followed her anxious gaze to a large door with Librarian written rather untidily across it.

I turned back to say something to the woman, but she was no longer there. Neither were there any people at the bookshelves, in the aisles or the tables, and the desk by the entrance had gone.

A terrible emptiness and silence pervaded the air.

Even though the scenery was the same and the skylights overhead showed a clear blue sky, I couldn't get rid of the feeling this was another room in that demented library and this one was a long distance from where I'd just been.

A very long distance.

There were aisles of bookcases crammed with postcards and there was a huge postcard expanded image on the far wall.

No doors led to another room though, and the photograph was different.

A far darker image of the town harbour peered out into the room.

There were figures in the streets and on the quay, but they weren't tourists. Their legs and arms and faces were too long and seemed to have been shaped from the late afternoon light that permeated the scene.

The longer I looked at these unsettling figures, the larger they seemed to become, as if they were bigger on the inside than the outside and composed of galaxies of tiny stars that grew more numerous by the second.

The image dominated the room, giving it an unnerving sense of otherness that sent me reeling.

Feeling as removed from the security of my own existence as is possible, I bent over and threw up a stream of bile onto the remarkably ordinary carpet.

When I regained myself I became aware that something now stood beside me.

As with the shapes in that distorted image, I felt a depth to this new presence that so raddled my perceptions I leant over and retched again.

Some wet papery extrusion took my arm and gave it a liquid squeeze.

It smelt of withered flowers, burnt bacon and wet dogs and although I only ever caught glimpses, I felt it was covered in glistening black bone, wore shadows and was too vast in presence to fit into my thoughts.

"Why does the little shell seek the original day?" It spoke with a voice like an approaching storm and hissed like flashes of lightning.

Answering with, "I was joking," didn't seem to make things any better. I kept looking up at the image and trying not to think it might at any moment turn into a mirror.

"You joke about the Endless day?" it asked. I realised the lecherous red light that was tearing apart my hearing was its voice.

"Endless? I thought you said the Original day?"

"Malaron and the Endless day sweep all before him. The painter of eons has worn his stars within our skies, little shell. Beware you listen without the spheres to guide you."

I hadn't a clue what it was hissing about but agreed with it nonetheless. My stomach was trembling like a frightened kitten and I knew if I threw up again it would not be pretty, or peaceful.

"How are your thoughts little shell?" it asked in a not unkindly way.

"Under pressure," I gasped.

"The spaces between are too vast for you to understand real language," it hissed and then a stream of rich melodic cadences assaulted my senses.

I heard a door slamming shut and the young woman was standing before me looking anxious.

The picture above the doors was of the crowds around the harbour and people were at the shelves choosing postcards.

I tried to be sick again but nothing came out.

"You should leave now," the woman said, "Librarians have effects."

I bet they did.

She gave a forced smile and handed me a postcard with a picture of the sea walls and tall painted houses resting above.

I thought about saying something amusing about overdue library tickets, thought better of it and left.

Outside I glanced at the postcard again and read the message on the back. It said, *"I think I'm from Littleway."*

I pocketed it and hurried away.

I stumbled down Smartscone Lane and into Air Street.

As if on cue, Mr Sand stepped out of the local newsagents carrying a copy of the Shellbridge Gazette.

He seemed amused to see me and I asked him if he had eaten any decent scones lately.

"You are mocking me," he said smiling, "I was not expecting to see you back so soon."

"And neither will you again," I told him, "this place is some sort of madhouse."

"That, Mr Pike, is open to interpretation. How are your drawings?"

"Of the orange man? How old do you think he is, Mr Sand?"

He opened the paper, showing me page three, and an article entitled, "Town Scholar Announces Orange Man One Thousand Years Old."

I stared at him.

Was Mr Sand a part of the madness that had infected this asylum?

"How long have you been here, Mr Sand?" I asked.

"Long? The space between two instants is infinite if you care to dissect it, Mr Pike." He seemed confused for a moment, then worked through either expression as if chewing something over. "Oh, five months to a day I suppose. It's been a trial, the place is such a puzzle, wouldn't you agree?"

I looked past him into the newsagents. An elderly figure in an apron better suited to a butcher was standing behind the counter. To one side I saw rack upon rack of magazines and newspapers. Stepping by Mr Sand, who for some reason smelt to me of something I'd eaten as a boy that had given me nightmares, I peered through the window.

All of the magazines had articles about the town, whether they were to do with gardening, fashion, sport or food, as did the *Seabridge Gazette*, *Seabridge Observer*, *Seabridge Herald* and *SeabridgeNews*.

I saw a doorway leading through to another room, also filled with racks of newspapers and magazines, and a further opening into a room beyond that.

"What have they got to write about?" I asked, turning back to Mr Sand, who was staring at his sandals.

"Oh you'd be surprised," he said without looking up. "How much time is there between two seconds? You know I've never been able to do feet."

I stared at him, seeing the odd papery creases in his skin and the strange way he stood, perfectly still one moment, all at sea the next.

"Unfortunately I have to go," I said, showing him my camera as if this was some strange farewell ritual.

"You've been taking pictures? Good," he said, looking up and no longer smiling, "I have no idea what the bloody things are. No one does. All colour and light Mr Pike, the shapes worthless, the sounds a mess. One would hope... but never mind."

He opened his paper and began to read so I gave up on him and moved away.

"You owe me a scone," he shouted after me.

It took an age to find the steps leading back to the road, as if the town had yawned and had a good stretch.

The coaches and their drivers slumbered on the road. The cars sat like row upon row of bright lozenges in the sun.

I turned and took some more photos of that curious town at the back of the bay, then left, hurrying now, back to my cottage.

On the way, I stopped off at one of the little beaches, sat down on a rock, and checked my camera.

A moment later I looked up at the gulls hovering over the waves and threw stones at them for mocking me.

Then, when I'd calmed down, I checked the photos again.

I hadn't been mistaken. These were the photos I'd taken, but every single one of them looked as though they were out of a guidebook.

As for the road that expired up on the scrub? No, this was a cheery picture of cars going by and a ribbon of tarmac stretching away to link up with the motorway.

I could almost see the caption underneath.

Some of the bloody things even looked like the images on the postcards I had seen.

There was not one image I had taken that looked real.

"Sounds like you've been taking the local mushrooms," Tim joked when I called him. "Or did you take some smoke with you in order to soften the blow of Marianne. She's been seen by the way, I think Oliver said she's was asking after you..."

"I'm not playing games," I said. "My camera's been tampered with. My mind's been screwed over and..." I realised how crazy I must have sounded so I swore instead.

The road had ended, I'd seen it.

He started laughing again and said he was looking forward to seeing the result of this new project I was dreaming up.

It was only after I put the phone down I remembered he had mentioned Marianne.

Why would she have been asking after me? We had agreed to part. Not in a friendly way either. After being accused of every single thing that was wrong with the world, I would not say amicably either.

She had smiled at that, "Bit childish isn't it Chris?"

Yes, I remembered that now.

Damn.

The sun was sinking and the clouds were melting in a flurry of yellow and crimson colours.

"You should be here," I said, *"you should be here watching this and telling me I am not going mad."*

I sat in The Hand and put on a decent impression of someone who had been roaming the coastal path and had been blown away by the wonderful scenery.

Or thought I did.

Andrew came in later and after complaining about the traffic on his way home ("like talking another language in this place"), mentioning the weather, and asking what I'd been getting up to, gave me a long hard stare and sighed. "You've been there, haven't you?"

I nodded.

"Ah well," he said glancing around to make sure no one was in earshot, "your mistake. Still moping over the loved one?"

The change of tack surprised me.

"I need her here with me."

"Then go back to the smoke, man, and find her." He was staring at me intensely. "Tell you what though, before you do that come out with me in the boat tomorrow, I'll show you those hard to reach coves I was telling you about."

After ordering another round of drinks he tried cheering me up by recalling disastrous relationships he'd had before he met Cathy. It was jovial enough, but I saw the way he looked at me at odd moments and knew his mind was elsewhere.

It was not until we were sailing away from the harbour in the small skiff the following morning that I remembered it was a Friday.

"Day off," he called from the back of the boat, grinning.

We emerged from the small bay and rather than turn west to follow the shore, we kept puttering on out to sea.

After some fifteen minutes of this, with the coastline a mirage of greens and greys I turned and gave him a questioning look.

He nodded and grinned.

"Not long now."

I looked around but could only see a calm sea and receding coastline.

To my surprise he then cut the engine and the boat began to drift.

"There," he said, and came and sat opposite me, "think we're far enough out now."

The boat moved gently in the light swell.

I wondered what he was talking about.

"Feel it?" he asked.

The boat rocked a little as he sat forward.

"Seabridge, Chris. How does it feel to you?"

"What do you mean?"

I listened to the waves as they slapped against the side of the boat.

When I thought about Seabridge my memories of the town were less clear, and I had the sensation of having dreamt of the place rather than actually having been there.

Andrew was staring at me the way the locals had on my first evening in Rainswood.

"Come on," he said in a determined voice, "you're getting it."

"Getting what?" I asked.

"The sea tends to absorb the effect. I think it's..." He looked out across the waves.

The smudge of land that had become the coast seemed an awfully long way away.

"I think it's the vastness of it all. Confuses the hell out of the locals when they're out fishing."

"What does?" I asked, becoming irritated.

"Seabridge," he said, "that little place you've been visiting the last few days. Never seems quite real when you're out here."

"It's real," I said, and told him of my experiences there.

After I finished he turned and looked down along the blur of land to where I presumed the entrance to the bay housing the town opened to the sea.

"You could hand me a million pounds and I still wouldn't risk my sanity visiting a place like that," he said, then gave me a stern look and added, "you must be mad."

"Is that what you've bought me out here for then? To tell me I've gone crazy?" I was getting a little pissed off with the quiet rocking of the boat and the intimidating sound of the waves slipping away around us.

"No Chris, I don't, but you might think I am after you listen to what I've to say. Then we'll both be crazy and can jump up and down and scream crazy things until we've calmed down, ok?"

I couldn't tell if I trusted this troubled geography teacher any more. He must have seen my expression because he put his hand up for quiet.

"Chris, six months ago Seabridge didn't exist. The land at the back of that squalid little bay was a swamp. It's the one area around here no one bothers visiting."

I stared at the mirage-like line of the coast.

"But I was there yesterday."

"So I gathered."

"So what do you mean?"

"I mean that out of all the people living in Rainswood, muggins here is the only one who drives a considerable distance to work and back everyday. Now mate I could go on and tell you about the stress of the traffic and the monotony of the drive, but that's for my wife to have to put up with. Instead, let's you and I step back to last November shall we?"

"If you say so," I replied.

"It was a Tuesday evening. I'd just driven past Oakhampton and some fifteen miles away from here when out of nowhere, and I mean nowhere, I remembered a place called Seabridge which was situated down the coast. It was vague at first, as if the name was treading water in my memory. As I left the motorway and approached Rainswood, though, it started to become, how can I say, more real. Each time I thought of the place I could see it situated at the back of that picturesque little bay. By the time I arrived home it seemed to me to be a part of the landscape. This wasn't a place I had just seen in guidebooks, Chris, I knew it as if it had been there ever since we had moved to Rainswood. I knew its history, the names of its landmarks, the sight of the harbour and the winding streets, all of it. And why not? Seabridge had been there ever since I'd found this part of the coast and we'd moved to Rainswood. Why wouldn't I remember it? But the feeling persisted of that area being a bog, and that no one ever went there. So I'm driving down the motorway with two versions of the same place competing for attention in my head. At first I thought I was going mad. But the nearer I got to Rainswood, the stronger Seabridge seemed to become, and I forgot about the marshland along the coast and accepted this picturesque fishing port for the real thing. When I mentioned it to Cathy, she said, 'Oh Seabridge? I was talking to Mrs Henderson about how it had sold its soul to tourism.' Then when I questioned her about what she remembered of the town she looked at me as if I'd gone mad."

He sighed. "You see, I've worked it out. There's a perimeter. I call it the radius of remembering. It's about twelve miles each direction as the gull flies. All the way to Oakhampton. Then the memory of Seabridge starts to fade away, and begins to feel like something you dreamed of the night before. In effect this makes me the sole executor of the marshlands that once existed there, because I'm the only one who can remember them..."

I stared at this large, boisterous figure with the wide smile. He was obviously having trouble telling me all this, just as I was having trouble taking it in.

If I hadn't found the termination of the coach road, or had that bizarre episode in the library, not to mention the bookshop, I might have thought him crazy.

"What really bothers me is that Cathy and the girls seem to think everything is perfectly normal. It's as if I'm living in some parallel universe or something. It's the same with the rest of the village. It's not important to them, and yet... I've seen one or two people pause when I mention the place, as if they're not certain. It's a trick of the memory, or they're tired, and they just accept it at that. That's why they like to test strangers by asking them about the place. It's an amusement. They bet on how long it is before people remember Seabridge. Yet there are no boats coming from that town, and no one visits there or vice versa. No one questions the place, Chris. Can you understand how it is, coming and going with that weird dream like remembrance hovering around all the time? It's maddening, and if you think I ever wanted to visit the place... after..."

He paused again and stared out across the waves.

"After what?" I asked.

"You know, the locals don't want to voice how they feel, in case people think they've gone mad. Recently I've noticed them becoming more bothered with the subject. It's as if the place is integrating into their lives so much they can't cope with what is happening to them. Rainswood is becoming suspicious of its memories, Chris."

We turned to look along the hazy outline of the coast.

"I want to get Cathy and the children out of here," he said quietly, "before something happens. How I can convince her, though?"

"You said... after...?" I asked him.

He looked at me a moment, "Watkins? Wilson? Give the man a name. I don't have one, just a distant memory of a figure who rented your cottage a couple of months ago. If I think about him enough I can just picture him about the cliffs. He had this long walking stick with a blue handle and I think he was a naturalist of some sort, but he's hazy now; it's as if I've dreamt him up. He might even be a figure from one of your paintings for all I know. Cathy hasn't a clue what I'm talking about and says she has no record of anyone staying in the cottage at that time. It's as though he's just faded out of existence... yet I'm sure he was here, and that he wandered around the coast and that he probably visited that bloody place... and that whatever happened there stole the memory of who he was, or is."

"I've seen him," I said suddenly remembering, "when I was at Mrs Perkins' tea rooms in Seabridge, there was a man at a table with a walking stick. He was staring at some postcards."

"Who, Wilson?"

I described what I remembered.

"Apart from the walking stick I can't say if that is Wilson," he said, "or even if his name is Wilson."

"He seemed anxious, as if he couldn't understand what was happening to him. Most of them do."

I remembered the message the woman in the library had handed me.

I had left out the more startling details of my visits to the bookshop and the Library – even now I wasn't sure I trusted my own memories of those curious events – but felt it necessary to tell him about the postcard.

"Buggered if I've heard of Littleway," he said after a moment. "Maybe it's another of those imaginary towns."

"What, you think there are others?" I asked.

"Chris I don't know what to think. Look, after Wilson, or whoever he was, faded from view, I began a dossier. It's under lock and key at the college. I take notes of any odd occurrences about Rainswood or Seabridge when I'm at home, go into work the following morning and put them in the dossier. It's all in longhand. Anything I put on my laptop goes awol when I begin driving away from, you know, the Radius of Remembering."

I could see he excelled in this act of bizarre espionage. As if spying on his local village, and passing his secrets to his other "outside" self, somehow helped him to tolerate what was happening.

"At least there will be a record of this, if anything happens to us..." His voice trailed off and he turned to look at the shore.

"Maybe it's a government experiment and it's gone wrong and they're trying to wipe our memories of the place." I said. "Maybe Seabridge did exist, something happened there and everyone in the place has gone mad and there are all these vapours in the air that are

making us... forget... or remember and..." I
remembered the library and shut up.

Chris slowly got to his feet and made his way to the
motor, "So it's all a dream then is it Mr Artist?"

"Everything's a dream," I said feeling the enormity of
the sea and wild currents around us, "maybe there are
weird vapours around here."

"And we're all going mad," he concluded, a wide grin
molesting his thick beard.

He started the motor and aimed the skiff towards
the coast.

We motored over to the hidden bays along the western
shore. He gave me a running commentary on the
geological make up of the area and for a time became
animated by his pet subject.

I saw landscapes of glassy beaches plagued with
unholy geometries and bestial vegetation while unholy
creatures emerged from the eons-ravaged shoreline.
But my sketches felt empty, and Andrew's voice lost its
passion as our thoughts again strayed back along the
eastern coast to the distorted siren's call of Seabridge.

We came into the harbour at Rainswood quiet and
subdued, and took ourselves to The Hand.

But the mood there was antagonistic, as if our
presence together reminded them too much of
Seabridge and all the confused thoughts that
anomalous town bought with it.

Although Andrew's usual good humour prevailed, I
felt a certain hostility and growing sense of paranoia
about these normally sedate and settled people.

We left early, the air outside the suddenly cramped
pub feeling fresh and welcoming.

Andrew stared at me a time, then put out his hand,
shook mine vigorously and said, "Be careful now."

I knew he would be going home to write down the

day's encounter, along with a full dossier on myself plus accompanying notes. I had seen him observing me at times during the day, as if referencing who I was, in case anything should happen.

Something in my manner must have communicated my intentions.

I spent the evening putting together my own dossier, a pictorial remembrance of what I had encountered. The Librarians and Mr Sand were hardest to recapture. Something about Mr Sand's expression annoyed me, as did the suggestions the Librarians had wings of some sort, which I had not been aware of at the time.

When I spoke to Tim it was as if he were on the other side of the world. Somehow my immersion in this damaged coast had removed all familiarity with my life in the city.

And he would not stop going on about Marianne.

People were annoyed with me for having to deal with her being in such a state. If I wasn't going to tell her where I was, he would.

I said I would get in touch the following day and that I was going to return sooner than expected anyway so everyone could stop worrying.

"Things have been getting a little bit strange down here," I told him.

"So you've got a new project. So bloody what. You need to clear up whatever the two of you have been arguing about."

"We split up, Tim. Ok. That's it in a nutshell. Oh and Tim? "

"What?"

"What does she look like?"

"Pardon?"

"I've forgotten."

And I had. Someone I dearly loved to see seemed to have slipped away from my mind. I kept trying to picture Marianne and all I saw were glimpses; as if I had dreamt up my partner.

He put the phone down on me.

The sky was still blue and smiling when I set off the following morning, but by midday a film of sluggish cloud had moved in along the coast and shut away the sun.

I sat awhile on the grassy bank beside the car park and sketched the town.

The cloud seemed thicker over the bay and lent the town a heavy cumbersome appearance, as if it had donned a large overcoat and was stepping outside.

I thought the Coach Hotel larger and more sombre. There were dim lights in the windows more suggestive of dusk and it sat above the town as though reasserting its supremacy in some sinister way.

To my left the cars slumbered in their familiar rows on the tarmac. I recognised them now, these abandoned metallic metaphors, just as I was familiar with the giant coaches lined up along the road.

Thrown up on the shore of this beleaguered town they had lost their meaning and I couldn't help but see them as ornaments, or pieces of a cruel puzzle I would forever be barred from solving.

The smell of fried food and warm pastry wafted across from the harbour to compete with the brine and seaweed scents of the bay.

I listened to the murmur of excited voices and the sound of the infant waves lapping against the bank.

It seemed to me then (and the ferocious sketch I then attempted evolved into one of my most disturbing paintings) that the waters of the bay were competing with the town at its head. That there was an insistent current working beneath the surface pushing against the harbour and sea walls as if resisting its approach, or, more surprisingly, attempting to force it away.

Seabridge, in contrast stood firm, its perspectives that day strangely distorted; the sea walls higher than I had seen them, the hotel above glowering, and the winding streets more numerous and the crowds more frantic, as if somehow taunting the water below.

Everything was either larger or smaller than I remembered from my previous outing. Had there been as many flights of steps? Were the houses as narrow and tall? Had the crowds been so frantic?

I walked passed the huge coaches, their smart green and black bodies rising above me like some strange new creature from the tropics.

In the front seats the pot-bellied figures of the drivers snored on, eyes shut fast, legs spread out, the sheets of whatever newspapers their dreams had led them from strewn across the floor.

Below the sound of the crowds came to me like a solitary blurred voice.

I stood by the steps and gazed down into the souvenir-obsessed scrum, faces anxious and excited as they rushed past taking pictures and scattering into and out of those small but cavernous gift shops.

The smell of warm pastry and sweetly sick odour of seaside rock charged the air like some new invading scent.

The flights of steps and ascending streets felt steeper, as if at any moment the town would rise up and wade into the sea.

I was drawing brief sketches on my pad, stealing small details to be relayed back to me later; the anxious face of a woman reeling back in the crowd as a fresh wave of shoppers emerged from a shop, waving souvenirs; a thickset man in sweat drenched shirt forever snapping his camera as if it had taken the place of his sight; an elderly gentleman in a black waistcoat being tossed about as if lost at sea; the grinning face of an orange man exploding from the upper walls of The Peaceful Waters Tea Rooms.

It struck me that some of the figures in the crowd might have been there during my previous visit.

I could not be certain; such was the frenetic onrush of the mass below. Neither did I want to join them to see if this were true. Even at the top of the steps the desire to do so was palpable, like some tourist call to arms.

Resisting the pull to join the cursed revelry of that demented mob, I followed the road a short distance, found another stairway and stepped into the less forbidding warren of back streets.

Here only the briefest of sounds – a footstep, closing of a door, whirring of a camera lens – was allowed entry.

I walked slowly through the knot of lanes; the pot-bellied orange gods above exploding from more walls than I remembered.

At the corner of Draught Street, I stopped to sketch some of these imposing figures before realising the fat grinning faces also looked familiar.

Mr Sand's ancient cult figures resembled nothing so much as the drivers asleep in the oversized coaches back on the road.

I looked at the houses from which they so innocently burst forth.

Was I was waiting for someone to step out of one of these narrow houses and explain to me why this would be so?

My hands shook as I hurried the last of these bizarre caricatures into my pad, uncertain now of anything this distressed town had to offer.

Andrew Winters' voice was in my head, calmly suggesting that now might be a good time to return home.

Instead I continued up towards the summit of the town.

I passed a newsagent's squeezed between two houses starved of any width.

Inside, the owner, a woman in an immense flowery dress sat surrounded by postcard stands. To the side racks of magazines and newspapers filled the walls and a doorway at the back gave onto another slightly smaller room, similarly furnished.

I spent a moment peering through the window at those receding rooms and doorways, all no doubt leading away to some singular place miles distant, where finally the headlines would talk of events on such an infinitesimal scale (they would be written in the language of other days and the magazines would feature articles detailing the minute lives lived in an infinite moment) they would excite about a solitary few seconds in the life of the most ordinary of men and ruminate upon the consequences as if they would shake the foundations of all things.

The woman was standing at the entrance showing me the headlines on a newspaper, which seemed to me to consist of numerical equations.

"The Teacher of the Bones is going to visit the Junior School," she said with a smile.

I turned and hurried away, up more flights of steps, along and into a narrow lane where the houses seemed to lean over to stare into one another's living rooms.

I climbed a steep cobbled lane that seemed to go on forever and where the parade of pot-bellied orange men seemed to leer down at me with a knowing look on their all too human faces.

Out of breath and disorientated, I came to the top of the town and at last stood before the dark brooding hulk of the Coach House Hotel.

A throwback to the age of the railway hotel (there being neither railway nor road, this should have awakened me to what followed), this morose and grimy edifice with its myriad dirty windows, dimly lit rooms, broken balconies and aging high-turreted roof seemed to rear up and cast judgement over the little fishing port below.

The smell of mildew and old seashells hung about the place like some deluded invitation.

I stood a moment before the flight of wide curving steps leading up to the huge opened doors, surprised and dazzled by the sharpness of the light spilling out from the reception hall.

From inside came the muffled sounds of voices and somewhere I swore I heard the whispering of some big band music.

I watched groups of visitors emerging from the maze of narrow streets below. As they began climbing a formidable flight of steps up to the hotel forecourt I saw them begin to pocket their cameras and the excitement drain from their faces.

In turn those other guests emerging from the hotel came out into the afternoon as if reawakened. The moment they were on the steps cameras were taken out and they became animated, pointing at the view and rapidly taking photos and talking excitedly.

It seemed to me, then, as if this bird's eye view of the town was less confused within its planning than I had originally thought. The copious twisted streets and almost vertiginous flights of stairs, high sea walls and long harbour walk and cramped surrounding streets, the huddled cottages and narrow houses, tea rooms and gift shops, suddenly fell into clean perspective; as if some invisible hand had suddenly wiped clean the whole and shown me the real picture.

I grew angry. Surely this was a joke?

The place looked, how could I say, planned.

As if someone were playing with this scenic town, or had built it at a whim – for whatever reason my imagination drowned in a hundred possibilities before retreating with the thought that it was all a trick of the light.

As I stepped into what I presumed was the lobby, a sense of disorientation seized me and I fell back and grasped the mildew-stained folds of a pair of large purple drapes.

The place was enormous; vast beyond belief.

I was standing on the edge of a chamber that seemed to go on forever. I could see neither ceiling nor far walls. Not that this would have caused much comfort.

Before me a vast black and white marble floor stretched off like some strangely mutated sea.

A smattering of old sofas, chairs and tables briefly created the pretence of a lobby.

A short distance away, rising from the empty floor like some dark panelled island, was a reception desk and offices.

Here absurdly tall figures in dark suits moved slowly, their small red eyes cold and unblinking, the expressions on their white mask-like faces one of scorn.

The whole area exuded a sense of servile menace.

Further back – a far more pressing madness now claiming my thoughts – another far taller figure, in a long green jacket, stood as if he were on guard, before row upon row of giant coaches, their long lines petering into a mist-veiled distance.

There must have been hundreds of them in that insidiously gargantuan space, one far too large for the dimensions of the hotel. Above me too the ceiling sank into a strangely luminescent sky, from which I now saw gigantic chandeliers cast a bright sheen over the chamber.

I found the staggering ineptitude of my reasoning to be toyed with.

And if good old honest reason couldn't cope I'd deal with it another way.

I became angry.

I watched as the stream of incoming guests walked wearily to the receptionists, handing over their carrier bags and gifts to those stalking mannequins, who then deposited them in a back room, and then returned and handed back a postcard – no doubt containing some insipid image and message pertaining to the town.

The exhausted figures then walked away down the lines of coaches to a chosen vehicle, climbed on board, made their way to their seats, sat down and fell into a deep sleep.

A few walked over to show the towering attendant their cards and he – he? I was and will remain baffled as to what this thing actually was – raised a long arm and with a hand larger than his questioner's head pointed to one of the row of coaches.

I watched this mad charade, feeling that within the comings and goings of the guests and those great long lines of coaches there lay a great secret only a loss of sanity would reveal.

My temper, call it impatience, that's my excuse, got the better of me. The whole thing was absurd, an affront to good reason. Crossing the floor, a journey of more time and distance than I'd given credit for, I came alongside the tall skeletally-thin attendant, who seemed not to notice me, although one of the receptionists was staring my way in complete disgust.

I became aware of the pungent smell of rust and overripe apricots, which came as a surprise, and there was a slight chittering noise about the towering figure. His skin was like paste, which his crude scowling features appeared to have been painted onto.

A silky metallic hiss crept from the slash of red lips.

"Esterone reveals. The light of bleeding rescues us from mayhem. Soon the lost night shall cause the heavens to rearrange their origins," it said, continuing to stare at the rows of coaches. "What does the frail shell want here? If it is not doing its artistry, it should scuttle back out of this reverential place before the stars drop down to seek the light of its blood. Now, frail shell, what do we think of that?"

It turned its face to stare down at mine and forced a cruel smile.

"Well?"

I've never been confident around tall objects. That's why there are so many in my paintings. I have a perpetual fear of their falling on me.

This thing was the size of a small crane but exuded a terrible sense of stillness I can still not recall without a shiver.

A man in green shorts, sandals and a khaki shirt appeared beside me and held out a postcard with an image of Mrs Perkins' Tea Rooms.

He turned it over and read from the back, *We had cakes and scones and they were the best I can remember. Henry thought the jam was out of this world, and Miriam recited one of her silly nursery rhymes.*

The Servant looked up and pointed to a row of coaches, then said, "Scram."

The man put the card in his pocket and walked off in the direction shown.

I became aware the Servant had turned to me again and I tried and failed to meet his cold gaze.

"I meant you, frail shell," it hissed.

"One thing," I said peeved at being insulted, "why do you smell of rust?"

It gave me such a look I turned and hurried back across the floor.

I knew then, these sinister servile apparitions did not look upon the same world I saw, and that their reason belonged to some other sphere of understanding.

When I got outside I stood in the forecourt staring down at the town and sheltered bay.

I followed the refreshed guests down the flight of steep steps into the narrow streets below.

Already I could hear their excited voices repeating holiday messages from whatever postcards they'd been handed at reception.

A growing chorus of banal observance, their meanings twisted with each repetition. An occasional challenge to these came from unlikely sources. A woman, with an umbrella I was later to see torn away in the human current down by the harbour, uttered words more in keeping with the attendant.

As she walked by she said, "Choose your place wisely, they told me, or the faceless waiters will arrive to feed you their expressions."

Her eyes betrayed her cheerful expression as she hurried by.

I entered Sleeve Street and followed these newly risen figures, watching as they became more excited by their surroundings.

How many times had they laid eyes on these rows of little houses and shops?

There was something in the way their pace quickened as they got nearer to the harbour; in the way they passed the parade of those returning to the hotel; in the way they took photographs of certain houses, rooftops and shop windows.

How they kept reciting those banal messages.

There was an insane symmetry at work, I realised. Stay in Seabridge long enough and the place would reveal itself.

It irritated me that I had been allowed to see this

insane harmony. I didn't want to see it. I didn't want to go back to the cottage and describe it in a painting.

It frightened me as much as those strange spidery receptionists and librarians had frightened me.

There was a reason for this, and it defied any form of reason I knew.

By the time I reached Neverline Lane, close by the streets surrounding the harbour, I thought I could see a pattern in the movements of these tormented souls.

I knew each of the shops I had passed contained more rooms than was acceptable; that the houses were vast repositories of the infinitesimal; that the post office would post any card or letter to nowhere but the town and that each message would pertain to the town; that every single item there somehow revolved around... what?

"You look quite upset, Mr Pike. Can I help?"

I turned to find Mr Sand standing beside me.

His smile was as paper-thin as the thing back at the hotel, his leathery skin just as mask-like.

"What's going on here?" I demanded rather stupidly.

"Nothing," he said looking around at the figures coming and going through the shops, "that you would ever understand I fear."

"Just what are you, Mr Sand?"

"Me?" he pointed to his dark frock coat and laughed. "I really haven't a clue, Mr Pike, and maybe that's the problem." He concluded this with a lowering anger in his voice and a look in his eyes I was steadily getting to know.

"What is this place then, and where are all these people from?" I was shouting because we were walking alongside one of the growing streams of figures hurrying to the harbour front. Although there was nothing overtly odd about their movements I detected in their growing excitement a sense of deep disquiet, of exhaustion and fear. The smell of sour clothes and sweat riddled the air. I saw broken sandals, damaged shoes, torn tee shirts and shorts.

"Everyone is on holiday," Mr Sand shouted, "they're all having a bit of a jolly. Oh what a wonderful time we are having. The hotel has lovely views." And he laughed, a loud baying laughter that made me want to punch him, although what good that would have done I don't know. He wasn't here, in these streets amongst these frightened crowds. He was somewhere where all this made sense.

I moved out of the crowd and out into a narrow alley.

"I'm going home," I said, "this is all a bad dream and you're like some cruel vicar leading his flock into a nightmare."

He shook his head, "I'm surprised by your reasoning. Whatever this is, it's not to do with your feast day religion."

"Then what the bloody hell are you, Mr Sand?"

His face seemed to contort. I could see Mr Sand the so called scholar and I could see something "other" and it was this "other" he was reluctant for me to see.

"It would take three of your days to perceive what I am Mr Pike, and two and a half of your months to recite my name. Fail to do so clearly and the surface of your sanity will be blown away like..." He hesitated then blew a loud raspberry and gave vent to a hideously provocative laugh.

I had no idea what he was, only that he was most likely beyond what I could reason, and that this entire fishing town was a part of him.

"There's a sickening harmony here," I shouted, "it's like some vast distorted symmetry. Am I right?"

He watched as a group of holidaymakers sped by taking pictures and mumbling messages from the back of postcards.

"No, it's not an illusion, fragile shell. Everything here is very real."

"Then where did you steal these people from?"

"I did not steal anything. They are mine to use. What you call people I see... How is this?" he screamed at me then, and uttered names that shook my senses rigid. "Do you know how difficult this is?" he said quietly, "trying to reason with a... with a thought...?"

I moved away, rejecting the pull of the growing crowd and trying to make for the harbour without getting caught up into the crowds that struggled there.

Mr Sand was walking beside me, although I hadn't seen him move from the alleyway. He was attempting to smile but his lips were trembling and his eyes were white as though he had gone blind.

"If I were you I'd accept my offer and have done with your stupid reasons," he said, "come on in the water's fine. Just last night we sat on our balcony and watched the stars. The fish and chips on the quay are the best we've ever tasted. The spheres are not friendly and neither are we. We are, outside of such things. I seek to understand who and where I am. You think you know and walk around inside your fragile shell full of benign confidence and understanding while the universe bleeds and dances beyond your capabilities. We are all pretty shells Mr Pike, only some are larger and from farther away than you can imagine. Now, will you take up our offer?"

"What offer?"

I could see the crowds turning into the harbour area. They seemed to me to be far more frantic than in previous days. I thought they were moving in a way beyond my understanding.

"We think an artist in residence might help us. Your imagination has rather a rosy glow. Don't worry, you wouldn't have to stay at the hotel, that's for the stolen.

You could have a cottage if you like. They're really quite big on the inside."

I stared at him as if he were some insane estate agent.

"I imagine they can hold up to a thousand rooms or more."

"Oh far more than that, if you've a mind to see. Which you do not, Mr Pike. Speaking with a thought is not... commendable, it's a bloody thing and causes a lot of ridiculous pain."

I thought of the exhausted souls returning to the sanctuary of the coaches and saw those same tired faces now, reinvigorated and hurrying to and fro, and wondered how they could keep this up.

"Who are these people?" I shouted.

"Part of an equation, Mr Pike, nothing more, merely parts of an equation. I removed them from their spheres. It uses a lot of energy to do so, but thoughts are necessary for our survival in this damnation of a universe."

"So you're not from around here I take it?"

He shook his head. "The question's irrelevant. I have no idea what here and around are. This sphere is not reasonable and neither am..." He stopped and shouted nonsensical names at me again. When he'd finished I thought I had probably lost most of the logic I'd grown up with and found I was crying.

He did not apologise and I found that all the time I'd known him, this was the only redeeming feature he had that corresponded to my own personality.

Everything else was beyond my reach.

"You've stolen these people," I said, "and are using them... look at Mr Wilson! I saw him absorbed by your ridiculous theorising. You can't just take people and steal their reality... surely there's some universal law that denies that?"

"Of course there isn't..." he said, "Why should there be?"

This was hopeless.

I followed the far edge of the crowd as it turned out into the harbour.

"I cannot be your artist in residence," I told him, "you'd only be having me paint images onto postcards, wouldn't you?"

"What's wrong with that?" he said, "you enjoyed the orange man figurines. We could have... what... quite a lot of fun... is that it?"

I swore.

I would never be able to understand what he meant by that.

I separated from the crowd and began to edge closer to the nearest jetty.

He followed, curious and with that dreadful paper thin smile on his face.

Behind him I could see the town crawling up the hill to the hotel and sensed all the visitors teeming about the streets, and about us, like ants, premeditated in their movements; dancing to some hellishly demented cosmic tune... a melody of postcard messages and blind photographic snaps.

There was a hideous harmony at work in that little town.

I turned to Mr Sand and threw my satchel and drawing books at him in a display of sulking.

He seemed taken aback as I ran along the jetty and dived headlong into the cold waters of the bay.

I wasn't sure what I expected – the town to break apart and some growling nether creature to come chasing after me; the crowds on the harbour to dive in after me; thunder and lightning; the sinister figure from the hotel to rise from the water and haul me away.

Nothing happened.

Once I had swum a suitable distance I paused to look back.

All was as it had been; the distant murmur of the crowd, the rushing bodies, dark hulk of the hotel above...

That insidious harmony had vanished though, and I could no longer hear those insipid messages voiced by the crowds.

I swam over to the grassy bank beside the car park and lay back in the returned sunshine.

After a while, clothes still sopping, I stood up and looked out to sea.

The coastline and sea felt comforting.

I found my satchel and sketch pads on a bonnet of one of the cars nearby.

There was a postcard on the top of the satchel with a drab picture of the harbour with a bleached sky and smattering of blank eyed tourists.

On the back in a scrawling hand was written, *"Wish you were here."*

And that was all.

I put it in the satchel and walked off back along the coast.

I think they found me halfway back to Rainswood.

That's as much as I could get out of Andrew Winters.

My experience at the town had taken more out of me than I thought. I was soaked to the skin, terrified, and disorientated. Somewhere back along that path I felt the entire coastline rise up around me and the sky fall in upon my thoughts.

I remember little after that and woke in my bed in the cottage two days later.

Andrew was in the room and a short middle-aged man with an elegant white beard was sitting on the bed and looking at me as if I'd just thrown up in his lap.

"You've been in the wars, haven't you?" he said and I replied, "I've been all at sea, doc, where are the lifeboats?"

He turned to a tall figure in a long leather coat standing behind him and said, "Bloody idiot's going to survive."

The other man, untidy black hair framing his long gaunt features, the most prominent of which was a large bone of a nose, stared at me with bright black eyes and smiled.

"Don't worry," he said, waving a pair of postcards at me, "you'll wake up soon enough."

I pointed to him and said, "There are a lot of inhospitable swans out there and you're one of them."

"I guess I must be," he said and burst out laughing.

I awoke a second time and Andrew Winters was alone in the room and it was night.

He pulled a chair close to the bed, looked through the open door to where I thought I could see his wife moving about the kitchen.

"It's gone, Chris," he whispered, "Seabridge is gone. No one remembers apart from us two. We have to keep it a secret."

I stared at him and said, "Where's it gone to?"

I awoke again and sunlight was streaming through the windows and Marianne was sitting reading a book in a chair beside my bed.

I stared at her a long time and said, "Are you real?"

She bent her head over mine so her long blonde hair fell about us like a curtain and kissed me.

"Is that real enough?" she said.

I hadn't a clue.

When I finally emerged from the fever they said had racked my senses for a week, another figure with a dark beard was sitting on the bed. He asked me how I felt and said I had suffered a complete mental breakdown.

I saw Andrew Winters and Marianne were standing behind him and Cath Winters was sitting in a chair looking tearful.

He prescribed a sedative but Marianne said she didn't agree with that so he said I just needed rest and as little excitement as possible, which they all seemed to find amusing.

I stayed awake for most of that afternoon, asking Marianne if she was really there.

After that I recovered at a reasonable pace.

I remember waking up beside her one morning and thanking Mr Sand for damaging my sanity enough to bring this wonderful vivacious woman back into my life, although that insane piece of cosmic indifference obviously did not have that in mind when we met.

And I found my wish with the two of us sitting on the terrace drinking wine and watching the sun slip below the melting horizon.

I managed a few confidential conversations with Andrew, although he had grown quiet and reserved, and seemed wary of anyone listening to us. He kept telling me that what they said about the marshes and the obnoxious odours that had quickened my breakdown and the delusions that I had suffered were an excuse, that he had found me raving on the path that afternoon and had felt something "other" seeping out from that malodorous bay.

How or why that fictional nightmare came to abandon us he wouldn't say, and his wife seemed puzzled when I mentioned the first doctor and his assistant to her.

When I asked about the postcard Mr Sand had left for me, Andrew said he'd never seen it. Neither did I find the one with the message from the woman in the library.

I returned to the city and continued to paint, and although there was still praise for my work, I found it lacklustre and uninspiring.

Marianne and I became engaged a year later and our past battles seem to have been forgotten.

She became protective of me, and rarely broached the subject of my dreaming fits.

Andrew Winters did not fare so well. Some months after we returned he wrote to tell me of his divorce, and that he had moved to Oakhampton.

He lost his teaching job because of his drinking and I received letters from him that made little sense.

He visited me, but Marianne was wary of him and said he was a bad influence.

By then he was rambling about all sorts of nonsense and the bored but cheerful teacher I had known had become a grim and confused figure. I lent him money and we remained in touch, although he would only write letters, saying his emails were easily manipulated.

Finally the letters dried up, and although I tried to trace his whereabouts he seemed to have disappeared.

About eight months ago, I received a letter.

He wrote to say he had recovered his wits and was settled "somewhere in Hampshire with like minds", and although these "like minds" appeared to indulge his peculiar obsessions, he no longer rambled on so cryptically and, if anything, had taken on a more authoritative air.

He would not tell me what he was doing but in one solitary confused passage, he said he had "followed the stairs to the shattered sea and been tortured by the wonders of the iron shore".

The words bought back a memory of something Sand had screamed at me that final afternoon.

Not long after I began to experience a series of flashbacks concerning my experiences in Rainswood.

Marianne blamed it all on my association with Winters. She said I talked in my sleep as if I was having a conversation with "some impossible being".

We quarrelled badly and a short time later, she again moved out.

I dug deep.

The dreams and flashbacks drained away as I confronted my fears in a series of paintings some have said are my best work and others scratched their heads over and wondered at my sanity.

"Size Traps Us All, Mrs Perkins", the exhibition which followed, was a critical success.

I am no longer known as the artist who "plays with things" but one who creates "bizarre unhealthy visions", which I find equally tedious.

Andrew Winters wrote to say he had visited the exhibition while he was on an "errand" in the city.

He spoke of my paintings as being "formidable beasts" and of my "creating something extraordinary and Other".

"It is certainly a different place than the one you once described to me. Those long sinuous streets almost seem alive, and the crowds appear as though they are being fed into them. And the expressions!

They look as if they're in the grip of some joyous terror."

But this was not the reason for his letter.

While he had walked around, "It seemed to me the visitors to the gallery were congregating in ever larger groups around those huge canvases and that, dare I say it, their behaviour began to reflect those of the figures in the paintings. Imagine my surprise when they began to take photographs and hurry en masse through the rooms, slowly merging with other groups.

"Could it be that your work contains something of the power of that frightful place?

"Would I be amiss in suggesting those visitors have returned to the exhibition over the following days?

"I fear something is taking place within the gallery, Chris, and that you need to do something about it."

I could take a hint.

I was being politely warned by Mr Winters and whomever he was working for.

To the consternation and surprise of so many, I closed the exhibition without explanation.

Most of the paintings had been sold to separate buyers and I assumed whatever "venomous tendencies" they possessed – Winters' words, not mine – had disappeared. I thought the paintings just looked absurd and only worked when they were displayed together.

I was called many colourful things for doing so, but that's never bothered me.

Some days later the owner of the gallery, thankfully still talking to me, brought around a postcard he said he had found on his desk that morning.

It was of a town square in some listless new town with a drab-looking fountain and bandstand and pedestrians standing around seemingly devoid of purpose.

A range of enormous snowcapped mountains,

appearing to have strayed in from another image, filled the background.

"Wish you were here", was written on the back and it was addressed to "The Artist In Residence".

"Anyone you know?" he asked.

I gave him my most sardonic smile – no doubt causing him to think I'd gone mad, which was probably close to the truth.

"Only too well," I said, and staring wistfully at the card, added, "It will take three days to perceive whoever it is, and their name is so incomprehensible it takes three and a half months to pronounce. Fail to do so will lead to the removal of your sanity..."

I don't think he believed me.

Anthony Thomson has an idea he lives in Brighton, but can never be sure. His short story "Burning Up" was published by ABeSea magazine. He's influenced by the paintings of Leonora Carrington and Remedios Varos, and he mines the soundscapes of sixties music for psychedelic nuggets.

The Quarterly Review

Reviews by Stephen Theaker, Douglas J. Ogurek, Jacob Edwards, Howard Watts and Rafe McGregor

Douglas J. Ogurek's work has appeared in the BFS Journal, The Literary Review, Morpheus Tales, Gone Lawn, and several anthologies. He lives in a Chicago suburb with the woman whose husband he is and their pit bull Phlegmpus Bilesnot. Douglas's website can be found at: www.douglasjogurek.weebly.com.

Jacob Edwards also writes 42-word reviews for Derelict Space Sheep. This writer, poet and recovering lexiphanicist's website is at www.jacobedwards.id.au. He has a Facebook page at www.facebook. com/JacobEdwardsWriter, where he posts poems and the occasional oddity, and he can now be found on Twitter too: https://twitter.com/ToastyVogon.

Rafe McGregor has published over one hundred and twenty short stories, novellas, magazine articles, journal papers, and review essays. His work includes crime fiction, weird tales, military history, literary criticism, and academic philosophy.

Stephen Theaker's reviews have appeared in Interzone, Black Static, Prism and the BFS Journal, as well as clogging up our pages. He shares his home with three slightly smaller Theakers, runs the British Fantasy Awards, and works in legal and medical publishing.

Audio

Life, the Universe and Everything, by Douglas Adams (MacMillan Audio)

Laughter beyond fits.

    Life, the Universe and Everything is a remarkable book, and not just for the cosmic pull-tab placed so aptly on its front cover. Like its predecessors it is an existential satire with vast and brilliant ideas. Like its predecessors it projects human foibles onto the whole of creation, thence to bounce back in a fatalistic and absurdly funny manner. And like its predecessors it indulges in a digressive, facetious and distinctly Adamsey disregard for the sanctity of traditional prose narrative. Unlike its predecessors it isn't really a *Hitchhiker's* novel.

    Capturing the internal zeitgeist of *The Hitchhiker's Guide to the Galaxy* and *The Restaurant at the End of the Universe* is, of course, impossible. Almost everyone who's read Adams has attempted at some stage to do so, and in almost all instances the attempt has proven at least moderately unwise. The person who came closest was – perhaps unsurprisingly, but then again perhaps not, given that he'd written *Hitchhiker's* as a duology and that the story wrapped up rather neatly at the end of the second book – Douglas Adams. But even the man himself found it something of a strain to replicate the freewheeling, towel-toting, mind-blowing hoopiness of what he'd set down previously. Less a continuation, more an inspired adlib sucked into the ravenous vacuum of unfulfilled publishing contracts, *Life, the Universe and Everything* is nothing short of a jump-started series reboot; a greatly laboured-over extemporisation that nevertheless is, as mentioned, quite remarkable.

The full scope of *Life, the Universe and Everything* is difficult to impart without going into the sort of detail

Volume Threein
THE HITCHHIKER'S GUIDE TO THE GALAXY

LIFE, THE UNIVERSE
AND EVERYTHING
DOUGLAS ADAMS
READ BY MARTIN FREEMAN

best served by reading the book. The basic storyline, however – the threads of plot used by Adams to connect the various dots and squiggles he'd laid down – is that of the people of Krikkit, a peaceful and isolated race whose sudden introduction to the wider universe provoked in them a xenophobic resolve to wipe out everyone who wasn't them. Thus came the Krikkit Wars, at bloody culmination of which they and their planet were locked away in a Slo-Time envelope until the end of days. Unfortunately, a cohort of bat-wielding Krikkit robots escaped incarceration and have been roaming the galaxy, ruthlessly reassembling the Wikkit Gate, which is the key to releasing Krikkit from its temporal prison. Should they succeed, the aforementioned end of days will take place somewhat earlier than the rest of the universe would like...

Even for those who know nothing of a *Doctor Who* pitch that Adams wrote for the BBC during Tom Baker's ascendency, entitled *Doctor Who and the Krikkitmen*, this underlying concern of *Life, the Universe and Everything* seems rather more like a problem in need of solving, *Doctor Who* style, than the sort of thorny bewilderment that *Hitchhiker's* regularly put out there for its quasi-heroes to blunder through, run away from or fail utterly to comprehend or even notice. Adams himself admitted to a certain frustration upon finding that none of his *Hitchhiker's* characters were remotely qualified to play the part of the Doctor; yet he persisted and – remarkably – found a way to compensate for and even make a virtue of the dearth of players. Ever the innovator, Adams told the story almost exclusively by way of digressions. More on this shortly.

At the conclusion of the first two *Hitchhiker's* books – and also the TV series – Arthur Dent and Ford Prefect are left stranded on prehistoric Earth, wistfully resigned both to the future destruction of the planet and to never finding a satisfactory question to complement the ultimate answer to life, the universe and everything. This is the natural endpoint of Arthur's journey, and from the unused draft chapters collected in Jem Roberts' Adams biography *The Frood* (Preface, 2014) it seems that Adams had tremendous difficulty writing him back into the story. He had, admittedly, done so once previously in Fit the Eighth of the radio series, but only through recourse to a second lightning strike from the infinite improbability drive. Having judged this unsatisfactory, Adams laboured until he came up with a wholly different *deus ex machina* solution, extricating Arthur and Ford from the antediluvian bathtub of prehistory and dropping them into the middle of Lord's Cricket Ground just in time for the Krikkit robots' first explosive appearance. Arthur subsequently travels in the Starship Bistromath (which is powered by restaurant physics), is abducted by Agrajag (a crazed bat-like incarnation of a creature whom Arthur has inadvertently killed many times over on the circle of life), learns how to fly (by throwing himself at the ground and missing), and faces off with a Norse god at an airborne party, none of which virtuoso pieces of Hitchhiker's lore seem immediately germane to the subject of Krikkit. In fact, Adams appears almost resentful of Arthur's lack of usefulness, and thus to be punishing him through a barrage of inventiveness that serves only to emphasise the qualities fostering that resentment. Arthur Dent, one of literature's most passive protagonists, becomes also one of its most passive-aggressive antagonists. Meanwhile, the story itself refuses to unfold. Except...

Somehow, it does. Amidst digressions that seem merely nostalgic, digressions that loop about themselves and come back together like tied shoelaces, digressions *within* digressions, which transpire to be not just digressions but indeed crucial plot points hiding in brazen anticipation of the big reveal, somehow the story of Krikkit is told. (And by this we mean not just the backdrop of Krikkit – which Slartibartfast exposits shamelessly – but the *actual* story; the saga of Krikkit once wrested away from the *Doctor Who* canon and repurposed for *Hitchhiker's*.) Arthur Dent remains totally ineffectual, Ford Prefect feckless and hedonistic, Zaphod a restless gadabout, yet through their free-floating conduit and surging by way of discursive slingshot, *Life, the Universe and Everything* takes on its own unique character. Adams, after dedicating the book, writes that it is "freely adapted" from the radio programme. The two words form at best an infelicitous understatement. In truth, and under cover of its irrepressibly zany content and an overly deliberate, at times predictable stylistic enunciation, the third *Hitchhiker's* novel was entirely retrofitted.

Nowadays, there are several different manifestations of *Life, the Universe and Everything* to choose from, not least of all an audiobook read by Adams himself (from which was taken his outrageously apoplectic posthumous contribution to the third *Hitchhiker's* radio series, voicing Agrajag with lisping, fang-tearing relish in Fit the Sixteenth). One such rendition that adds definitive nuance to Adams' text is the 2006 audiobook read by Martin Freeman, who in 2005 had played Arthur Dent in the film version of *Hitchhiker's*. Not only does Freeman exhibit a well-pitched array of character voices, he brings also a dash of his more assertive film persona to the narration, the story thus coming across almost as if filtered through the perceptions of a more rounded, more self-assured Arthur Dent. If *Life, the Universe and Everything* has garnered one particular criticism it is that, unlike the seat-of-the-pants exuberance of its much-vaunted predecessors, its word follies, for all their careful construction, feel inexplicably piecemeal. Freeman's contribution goes a long way towards plastering over the cracks in the façade.

All told (and as frequently related in this review) *Life, the Universe and Everything* is a remarkable book. Perhaps not *wholly* remarkable – perhaps not reaching the fanciful heights of perhaps the *most* remarkable book ever to come out of the great publishing corporations of Ursa Minor – but remarkable nonetheless, and even more so as read by Martin Freeman. Thirty-four years on, pulling the ring-tab will still open to readers a novel of largely unparalleled zest. *Jacob Edwards*

Books

Jacaranda, by Cherie Priest (Subterranean Press)

Juan Rios is a nineteenth-century padre with a past painted in blood, some of it spilled righteously, most of it not. He has the power to Look and Listen, to see and hear more than others, and his involvement in many queer events, such as the incident at Rose Hill and the rancher at Four Chairs, has given him quite the reputation. That's why Sister Eileen asks him to come to Galveston, Texas, to investigate the deaths at the Hotel Jacaranda, built against the pleas of the locals on the site of an ancient jacaranda tree. By the time he gets there, everyone else is leaving – there's a massive storm on the way, one with a fair chance of flattening the hotel altogether. Almost everyone, anyway. There's a bunch of people still at the hotel, visitors and staff, who couldn't bring themselves to leave, and the hotel has been *talking* to some of them. It hasn't been saying nice things. As the storm draws close and the bodies pile up the book traps the reader in the hotel too, listening to the tiles being ripped from the roof and the whispers from the spiral on the floor. This novella is part of the Clockwork Century series, like *Clementine*, reviewed here a few years ago, set in an alternative version of old America, but it's very different. Where that was a rip-roaring tale of airships blasting each other out of the air, this is a

tense story of people under siege, physically and psychically, under a roof that's likely to fall down upon their heads, but it's it's just as good. Peculiar Sister Eileen and the padre make an interesting pair of protagonists. *Stephen Theaker* ★★★☆☆

Lone Wolf 21: Voyage of the Moonstone Collector's Edition, by Joe Dever (Mantikore Verlag)

I wonder if (m)any readers remember the thrill of picking up *The Warlock of Firetop Mountain* for the first time? Of realising that they hadn't lost their thread in the real world, but were lost in the maze under the mountain? Or of not realising they were in the maze until the appearance of the deadly Minotaur? *Firetop Mountain*, the brainchild of Steve Jackson and Ian Livingstone, was the first Fighting Fantasy gamebook, published by Puffin in August 1982. The series was a great success, with fifty-nine books available by 1995. The first instalment nonetheless remained the most popular, spawning two sequels – *Return to Firetop Mountain* (#50, 1992) and *Legend of Zagor* (#54, 1993) – various spin-off products, and reprinting as late as 2010. I find it difficult to convey the excitement of Fighting Fantasy to twenty-first century readers, but one must remember that they appeared in a decade without the internet or household computers, where "TV games" (for those who could afford them) were restricted to Pac-Man and Space Invaders. Unlike the *Choose Your Own Adventure* series, which was well underway when *Firetop Mountain* appeared, Fighting Fantasy was aimed at young adults rather than children, with the best adventures combining compelling storytelling with pleasing terror at what awaited in the next numbered section. I must have played *Firetop Mountain* for the first time in 1985 or 1986, but quickly

left Fighting Fantasy for a newer series. Lone Wolf was
written by Joe Dever and launched with *Flight from
the Dark*, first published by Sparrow in 1984. Where
Fighting Fantasy were all standalone adventures, some
of which took place in different universes, Lone Wolf
adventures were self-contained but constituted an
extended quest by a single character who progressed to
new levels of expertise in a vividly-drawn and complex
world called Magnamund. The epic began with the
extermination of the Kai – an order of warriors
dedicated to protecting the nation of Sommerlund as
well as the rest of the free (medievally-speaking) world
– at the hands of the demonic Darklords of Helgedad.
Readers adopted the persona of Kor-Skarn (Lone
Wolf), the sole survivor of the Darklord attack, and his
first mission was to convey the bad news to the king.
The missions became gradually more challenging as
Lone Wolf advanced in power and ended up with the
destruction of the Darklords in *The Masters of
Darkness* (#12, 1988). The road to Helgedad and
beyond was a rocky one, however, no more so than for
Dever himself.

    The first sign of the troubles ahead began between
books 7 and 8, *Castle Death* (1986) and *The Jungle of
Horrors* (1987), when Dever had an acrimonious split
with his illustrator. Once the Darklords were destroyed
and the (New Order of the) Kai re-established, there
seemed little work left for Kor-Skarn, but Dever
launched the Grand Master series with *The Plague
Lords of Ruel* in 1990. Although readers continue with
the same character, who had by now reached
unprecedented levels of power, there was no
overarching epic quest and each new adventure saw
Lone Wolf troubleshooting evil in a previously
unexplored region of Magnamund. I must admit my
interest flagged a little at this stage – partly due to my
age, no doubt, but also because I found the individual

missions something of an anti-climax after the
extended campaign of the first dozen. If some, like
me, left the fold temporarily, replacements must have
been pouring in as the Grand Master series raced to its
conclusion in *The Curse of Naar* (#20, 1993). Kor-
Skarn's powers were now demigod-like and Dever did

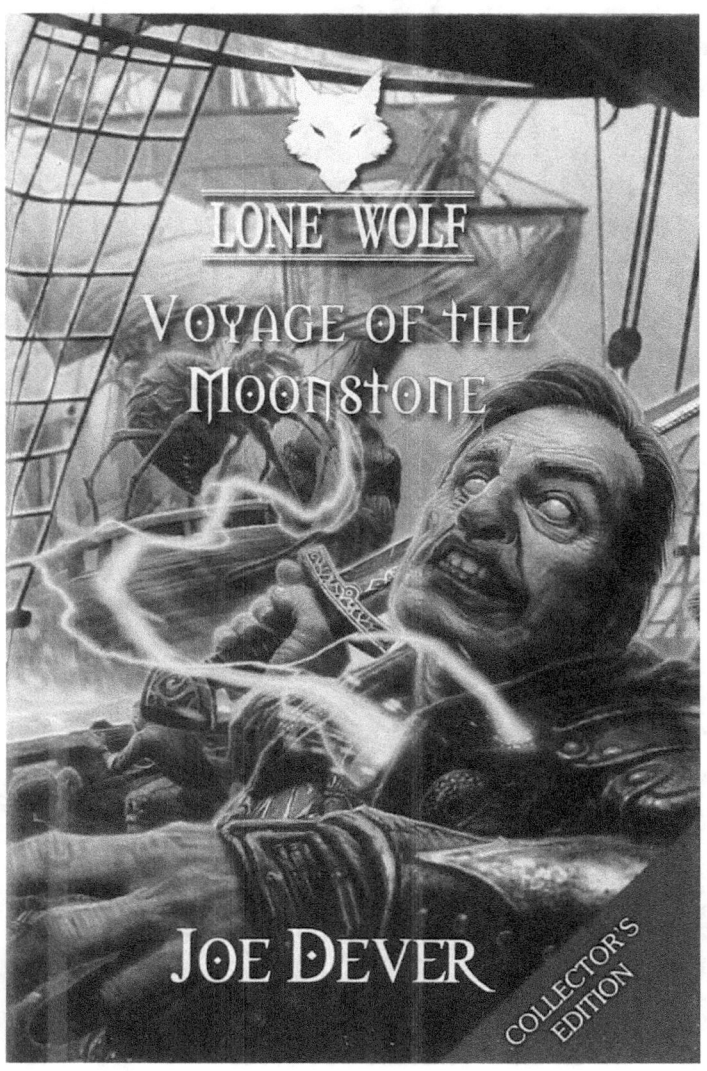

something risky but astute, introducing a new persona for readers. Twelve books were planned for the New Order series, beginning with *Voyage of the Moonstone* in 1994. The second New Order adventure, *The Buccaneers of Shadakai*, was published in the same year, but Red Fox had concerns about the internet-technology-inspired loss of interest in gamebooks and dropped Dever after *The Hunger of Sejanoz* (#28, 1998).

Dever then made another wise decision, authorising a group of enthusiasts calling themselves "Project Aon" to upload all of the gamebooks as free ebooks in various platforms, i.e. used precisely the technology that had killed the series to maintain interest. Such was the fan base that all twenty-eight books were made available over the next fifteen years (Project Aon completed in 2014 and can be found at www.projectaon.org). In the interim, the secondhand market for Lone Wolf paperbacks went berserk. There had been some problem with the publication of *The Buccaneers of Shadakai*, the result of which was that it sold out almost immediately in 1994. Five years later, copies were selling for hundreds of pounds. I confess to spending the most I have ever spent on a book (£200) at a time when I really couldn't afford it (1999) to acquire a copy (left on my town centre doorstep by the postman). A new copy of the same paperback is now going for £999 on Amazon. The final instalment is currently the most sought after: *The Hunger of Sejanoz* varies between £699 and £999 for used copies.

The gamble with Project Aon seemed to pay off in 2004 when Mongoose Publishing launched a Lone Wolf Role Playing Game. The following year, however, Dever underwent surgery for cancer and was out of the public eye for some time. In 2010, with Dever fully-recovered, Mongoose announced that they would republish all the Lone Wolf books in a hardback

Collector's Edition, with new illustrations and fresh revisions by Dever. The books were priced at about £15, very reasonable given the quality of the covers, paper, and binding, and Mongoose furthermore offered a Megadeal: all twenty-eight plus the previously unpublished books 29 to 32 for something like £300 (a substantial saving). Despite my previous profligacy I was wary, having been burned by small presses before (and since). I was initially proved wrong, with seventeen books released in three years, but there was a lull of a few months in 2012 and the following February Dever announced (via Project Aon) that he and Mongoose had split by mutual consent. Two further announcements followed in quick succession: the German Mantikore Verlag would be publishing books 18 to 28 (in English) in the same Collector's Edition format (March) as well as the final four volumes (April).

Mantikore published book 18, *Dawn of the Dragons*, in May 2013 and began the New Order series with the Collector's Edition of *Voyage of the Moonstone* – which this review is supposed to be about – last year. *The Buccaneers of Shadakai* was also published in 2015 and I have found them easiest to acquire via Amazon (rather than the publisher). The books appear to automatically revert to "unavailable" on the publication date, but can be bought at the same price (still £15-odd) via secondhand sellers (at least one of which is based in Germany). Regardless of what's going on behind the scenes, all my Mantikore edition purchases have been entirely satisfactory – purchased more for support than anything else as the first gap in my collection is book 25. I'm not completely convinced I'll ever hold a copy of *Trail of the Wolf* as publication appears to have slowed down again, although cover artwork is available for *Mydnight's Hero* (#23) and *The Storms of Chai* (#29). According to Wikipedia, the series (published in numerous languages – there are three on Project Aon alone – and including numerous spin-offs) has sold eleven and a half million copies worldwide, but the real figure must be considerably higher given all the craziness on the secondhand market.

Voyage of the Moonstone begins thirty-three years after *Flight from the Dark* and readers must create a new character by use of the series' standard method, a random number table. I'm afraid my New Order warrior has the rather delicate name of True Friend, but he is a Kai Grand Master, can kill you with his bare hands, live off the land indefinitely, and move small objects by looking at them, so you'd better not tease him about it. True Friend's first mission is to return the magical artifact called the Moonstone (with which readers of the series will be familiar) to its rightful owners on the Isle of Lorne. One of the reasons Dever's decision to reboot with True Friend was shrewd is because it does away with the only consistent criticism of books 3 to 20: that they are either too easy or too hard, depending upon the combination of whether one acquired the Sommerswerd (the broadsword to end all broadswords) at the end of *Fire on the Water* (#2, 1984) and one's Kai level (determined by the number of books one has previously completed). I think the critique is overly harsh because I picked up the Sommerswerd on cue, but remained far from invulnerable – aside from which there are various other magic weapons to be found in unlikely places. Notwithstanding, True Friend has no such problems, carrying no Sommerswerd and with no previous adventures counting towards his skills.

Given my emotional and financial investment in Lone Wolf, I can hardly do anything other than recommend *Voyage of the Moonstone*. I shall, however, say that although the first New Order adventure is as good as many of the originals (and perhaps better than several of the Grand Master series), the finale – always a single combat with a particularly nasty denizen of Magnamund (or the Daziarn Plane) – is a little disappointing. The Otokh is a giant lightning-spinning sea-spider (depicted on the cover), which sounds sinister as I type, but wasn't quite as menacing as some of the antagonists I've dispatched with the Sommerswerd. A regular feature of the Mantikore editions has been the inclusion of a bonus mini-adventure and the first New Order Collector's Edition continues this practice with a return to Kor-Skarn entitled "Echoes of the Moonstone" (written by Eberhard Eschwe and Swen Harder). This is an unusual choice, subject to the problems noted above despite having a strategy for dealing with them, but is close to the main adventure in length so the reader at least gets two for one. *Voyage of the Moonstone* ends midway through the mission such that it is not clear whether True Friend will end up on an epic quest of the likes of his master's early years or take over as Magnamund's chief troubleshooter. The mission continues in *The Buccaneers of Shadaki* – going for a song at £13.71. *Rafe McGregor*

Patchwerk, by David Tallerman (Tor.com)

Scientist Dran Florrian has sneaked on to the TransContinental, in the cargo hold of which is his great invention, Palimpsest. The result of five years of work and a lifetime of thought, it is too powerful to be in the hands of a ruthless weapons man like Harlan Dorric, who is waiting for him in the hold. Also there, two hired guns, a technician who blocks Florrian's neural connection to his clever machine, and Karen, the wife he lost while buried in work. Hang on, no,

that's not right. He's D'ren Florein, on a queenship, an
intelligent insect trying to counter the Nachtswarm,
entomological engineering gone mad, and Halann
D'rik is the one trying to take control of Palimpsest.
No, wait, that's not right either... This is a good novella

Sometimes
all you need
is an infinite
number
of heroes.

PATCHWERK

DAVID TALLERMAN

that could easily have sprung from one of the Baen collections of classic science fiction by Poul Anderson or Murray Leinster, but instead it's from David Tallerman, one of our own past contributors. He thinks up lots of neat tricks for the protagonist, whatever his name at any given time, to play with the Palimpsest, weaving a sharp little thriller through the middle of it. So far, the Tor.com line of ebook novellas is living up to expectations, and my expectations were high. *Stephen Theaker* ★★★☆☆

The Sign in the Moonlight and Other Stories, by David Tallerman (Digital Horror Fiction)

David Tallerman has achieved not only remarkable but rare success with his short fiction. In the space of nine years, he has had more than seventy-five stories published in venues such as *Clarkesworld*, *Interzone*, *Alfred Hitchcock's Mystery Magazine*, *Andromeda Spaceways Inflight Magazine*, *Lightspeed*, *Nightmare*, *AE*, *Chiaroscuro*… and of course *Theaker's Quarterly Fiction*. This is his first short story collection – the appearance of which is itself an achievement given the reluctance of publishers to take on such projects. The short story came into its own with the rise of literacy in Europe and North America during the nineteenth century, but declined dramatically with the rise of domestic television ownership during the twentieth century. In the second decade of the twenty-first century, it is easy to forget that many of the most famous speculative fiction writers – Robert A. Heinlein, Ray Bradbury, Isaac Asimov, Philip K. Dick, and even Stephen King – began their careers as writers of short fiction. The notion of supporting oneself financially by short fiction alone is already archaic and authors like David (and publications like *Theaker's Quarterly Fiction*) breathe life into what might otherwise be a dying art form. I must interject a disclosure (or perhaps disclaimer) before I proceed: I met David while he was living in York and was surprised to discover that he had been kind enough to dedicate *The Sign in the Moonlight and Other Stories* to me in memory of the small assistance I was able to give him with the initial drafts of some of the stories. Our acquaintance has not prevented me from writing this review, however, because my primary concern is not the quality of the stories. That has already been judged by others: thirteen of the fourteen have been previously published – in *Andromeda Spaceways Inflight Magazine*, *Nightmare*, *Flash Fiction Online*, *Necrotic Tissue*, *Bull Spec*, *Bards and Sages Quarterly*, Angry Robot's blog, and three anthologies – with "War of the Rats" appearing for the first time.

The collection makes several hard to acquire or out of print publications available again, most notably "The Facts in the Case of Algernon Whisper's Karma" from *The Willows* and Spectral Press's "The Way of the Leaves". For this, Digital Horror Fiction (which is an imprint of the Digital Fiction Publishing Corp) should be praised, as well as for selling both the digital and paperback editions at reasonable prices. The publisher is nonetheless the target of my main criticism, which is that the paperback appears to have been deliberately extended across as many pages as possible. The font is on the large side of medium and the lines are double-spaced, so that even a work of flash fiction (the excellent "The Desert Cold") is stretched over four pages (six if one counts the illustration). Each story has its own black and white illustration, by the talented Duncan Kay, on a verso page but the respective recto pages have been left blank and there is altogether too much white space between front and back cover. What puzzles me is that if there was a need to increase the page count – and I understand that there often is for a variety of reasons – the publisher didn't include more of David's stories. There are plenty to choose from – "Devilry at the Hanging Tree Inn", published in *Theaker's Quarterly Fiction* #37 (2011), to take just one example. Kay's illustrations provide an impeccable complement to the stories,

from first ("The Burning Room") to last ("The Way of the Leaves") with no exceptions. Where they are particularly successful is in the pictorial representation of the way in which David mixes the literary with the pulp uses of language. Kay offers David's readers a mirror in which the pitch of each story is perfectly reflected, from the humour and self-conscious playfulness of "My Friend Fishfinger by Daisy, Aged 7" to the sophistication and seriousness of "Prisoner of Peace". Kay has also pulled off another balancing act, revealing enough of each tale to tease his audience while expertly avoiding spoilers in a completely harmonious match between illustrator and author.

The Sign in the Moonlight and Other Stories is introduced by Adrian Tchaikovsky of Shadows of the Apt and insect-kinden fame. Commenting on the theme of the volume, he writes: "Every story here opens a door onto some human trauma: loss, grief, death, murder and madness, encounters with the horrors of the supernatural and perhaps the worse horrors that simple mundane world can inflict" (p. 2). I'm not sure whether his description is accurate. If it is meant to indicate a distinctive world-view, in the sense that S.T. Joshi takes as definitive of the weird tale as opposed to other categories of speculative fiction, then not because there is no consistent *gestalt* that underpins these stories. If it is meant to indicate that all of the collected stories belong to the horror rather than fantasy or science fiction genres, then Tchaikovsky is correct and whatever else they achieve, they inspire the right combination of the fear and disgust that one demands from the tale of terror traditional or contemporary. The absence of underlying world-view does not detract from the unity of the volume; one of its strengths is the way the stories criss-cross the style and substance of subdivisions within the genre – gothic romanticism, the English ghost story, and the cosmic weird to name but three. The collection is to my mind well-named: "The Sign in the Moonlight" is my favourite story, where fact and fiction combine to produce a tensely entertaining tale inspired by – rather than a slavish pastiche of – the themes explored by H.P. Lovecraft. My only disappointment is "A Twist Too Far". The narrative is accomplished enough on its own, and was no doubt an asset to the issue of *Andromeda Spaceways Inflight Magazine* in which it appeared, but is eclipsed by "The Facts in the Case of Algernon Whisper's Karma" here. The stories are quite similar and the latter is superior in both intrigue and ingenuity. A minor complaint in a collection that is a major success. *Rafe McGregor*

Comics

Brightest Day, Vol. 1, by Geoff Johns, Peter Tomasi and chums (DC Comics)

At the conclusion of the Blackest Night, where Black Lanterns had laid siege to Earth, several dead heroes and villains were brought back to life by a blinding white light. Among them were Hawkman and Hawkwoman, Hawk (of Hawk and Dove), Aquaman, Martian Manhunter, Captain Boomerang, the Reverse Flash, Osiris, Jade (the original Green Lantern's daughter), Firestorm and Maxwell Lord, the psychic who once brought together the Justice League International. It also brought back one character who had been dead since his debut, Deadman, who will presumably need to change his name now. This book follows them all as they adjust to being back in the world, and in the case of Hawkman and Hawkwoman, out of it in what seems to be another dimension. I'm

not a particularly huge fan of any of these characters,
and I wasn't even aware that half of them were dead,
so their return to life didn't get me all that excited, but
it was very good fun to read a DC comic that followed
a bunch of characters in its universe without jamming
them together into an ad hoc group. It's a network
drama of the DC universe, letting their stories unfold
and bringing other guest stars in as the story demands

it. There's a connection, the light that brought them back having coalesced into a white lantern, which sends Deadman off to check in on each of the others, but each storyline gets its own room to breathe. The art does its job well. It's very gory at times, with people being stabbed and skinned, and one incident (on a ship) is very unpleasant in a different way (even if Aquaman and Mera do come to the rescue), so this isn't a book for children. People who have read quite a lot of DC comics are likely to get the most out of it. *Stephen Theaker* ★★★☆☆

Days Missing, by Phil Hester, Frazer Irving and chums (Archaia)

The Steward is a white-haired guy who fights like Neo and (theoretically) exists outside of time in a colossal library, watching our world go by. When a particularly disastrous day comes around, he steps in, to inspire people, to fight them, to cover up his own existence, and presumably sometimes just to relieve the boredom of spending eternity on his own. If he can fix things before the day is done, smashing, but more often he has to rewind time by twenty-four hours and reshape events. It's as if Bill Murray in *Groundhog Day* learnt to activate his time-looping ability on demand. The day lost in the loop may echo in the feelings and dreams of those that live on – for example, Mary Shelley in one story, whose encounter with a reanimated corpse inspires *Frankenstein* – but otherwise the only record of that lost day is in the books that line the Steward's library. He was alive before humanity existed, and seems likely to long outlive us, but he'll do his best to keep us going. Do you have any idea how long he spent trying to talk to dinosaurs before we came along?

This is a slightly odd book, that feels like it is

intended as a sales document for a television format as much as a comic: the rather foggy premise (which I didn't understand until it was all set out very clearly in the last issue) was cooked up by Roddenberry – not Gene Roddenberry, but Roddenberry the company, run by Gene's son and his friend Trevor, who have then

pulled in a variety of creators to produce the individual stories, much like writers and directors coming in to produce individual episodes of a television show. Once I realised that, I expected it to be poor, and yet it ends up being fairly decent. The hired guns include people like Phil Hester, Frazer Irving, Dale Keown and Ian Edgington, and the stories they produce range from the okay to the actually pretty good. The best comes last, with the Steward stepping in to rewind time nine times over when an accidentally-created artificial intelligence makes plans to devour the planet. It's rather chilling when he tells the laboratory staff how long it usually takes each of them to give in to madness, and Frazer Irving's artwork really sells it. Other stories feature conquistadors, the Large Hadron Collider and an outbreak of ebola. Worth a read if it comes your way, but don't seek it out unless the premise particularly appeals. *Stephen Theaker* ★★★☆☆

Ex Machina Book One, by Brian K. Vaughan and Tony Harris (Vertigo)

The mayor of New York isn't a Republican or a Democrat. He was a superhero, and before that an engineer, sent to investigate something weird and green glowing underneath the Brooklyn Bridge. Whatever it was blew up in his face, and he gained the ability to talk to machines and (perhaps more usefully, since we can all do that) have them follow his instructions. He grew up reading Justice League of America comics, so naturally, with the addition of a rocket pack, helmet and alien blaster, he became the Great Machine. It didn't go very well, and after his secret identity was blown he decided to run for mayor, to put himself in a position where he could effect real change. He won, though not for reasons he would ever have wanted, and now he's trying to run a city where psychos want to kill him, the commissioner of police and the state governor both hate him, and a publicly-subsidised gallery is about to display a painting of Abraham Lincoln with a racist word scrawled across his chest. His powers are only going to help with *some*

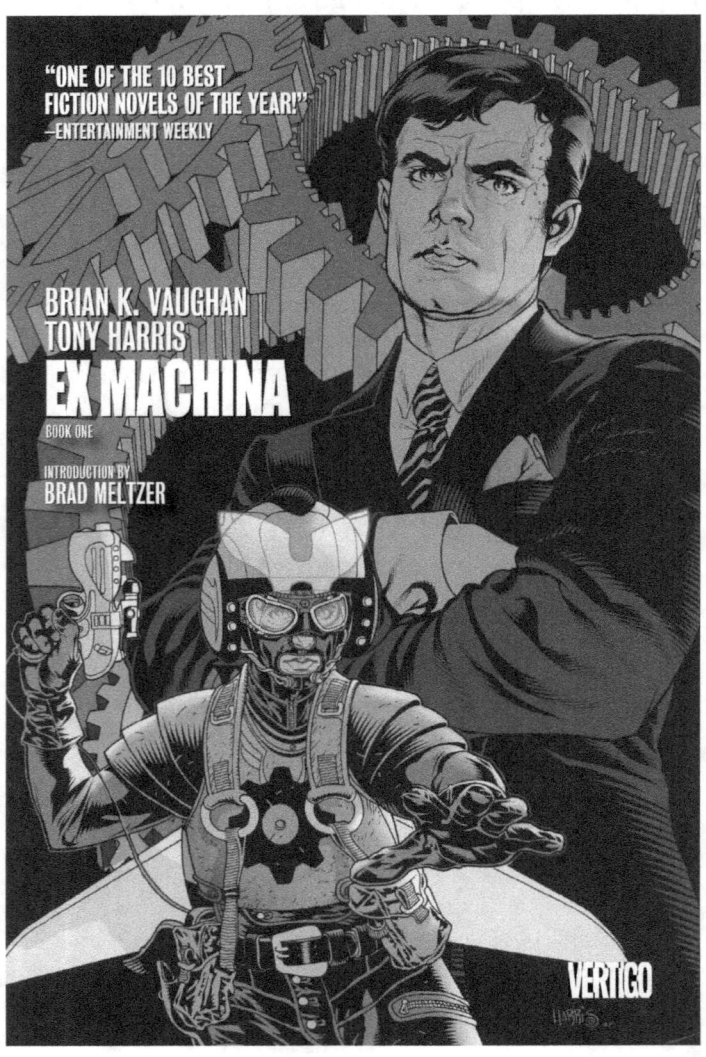

of those problems. This 273pp book collects the first eleven issues of the original comic, and it got off to a terrifically confident start. The narrative bounces around the mayor's timeline without ever confusing, and mixes ongoing plots with shorter self-contained stories with an apparent ease that must have required a good deal of work. The artwork is striking and unusual, looking almost as if photographs of actors have been rotoscoped to produce it. However it was produced, the result can be peculiar, but only because it has led to such a surprisingly varied range of expressions, faces and poses. I'd read parts of this book before, out of order, borrowed from the library, but it's a real treat to start from the beginning, knowing I have books two to five waiting to be read in my Comixology library. The entire set cost me just £15 in a sale. I won't often get the chance to spend my money more wisely. *Stephen Theaker* ★★★★☆

Goldtiger: The Poseidon Complex, by Guy Adams and Jimmy Broxton (Rebellion)

Lily Gold and Jack Tiger are fashion designers at London's most stylish fashion house, Goldtiger, but have a side project: adventure. In this book, collecting newspaper strips which supposedly appeared in the *Maltese Clarion* during the sixties, they investigate the disappearance of a number of boats on the Thames. Eventually this will lead them to the carnivorous Mr Sobek, but before then the putative artist of the strip, Antonio Barreti, will get bored of the scripts provided by Louis Schaeffer and begin to draw whatever the heck he likes, to the point of inserting himself into the story. In reality, this is the work of Guy Adams and Jimmy Broxton. The idea of the book is neat, and the strips do a good job of recreating the feel of the actual Modesty Blaise or James Bond strips from that period.

But there are so few of them: by my count just eighty-nine finished strips, appearing two to a page, which means they only fill about a third of the book, the rest being substantially padded out with text pieces, photographs and rejigged pieces of art. The Goldtiger adventure is okay, but there's never time to get into it, while the text pieces spend a lot of time telling us how outrageous and shocking the strips are, which the strips don't really live up to. It was a potentially interesting project, and you can see why it picked up plenty of backers on Kickstarter before finding a home with Rebellion, but it feels half-finished and scraped together. That may be deliberate, all part of the gimmick, but readers who like the sound of it will probably have more fun with Modesty Blaise herself. *Stephen Theaker* ★★☆☆☆

Predator vs Judge Dredd vs Aliens: Incubus and Other Stories, by John Wagner, Andy Diggle, Henry Flint, Alcatena and chums (Rebellion/Dark Horse Books)

Judge Dredd and his fellow lawmen here face two

extraterrestrial threats from the silver screen. In the first story a Predator crashes in the Cursed Earth, and from there makes his or her way to Mega-City One, where four hundred million people are already losing their minds. The Predator quickly realises that the judges are the big game here, and begins to collect its gruesome trophies. A somewhat psychic descendant of

Arnold Schwarzenegger's character from the first film is called in to help in the search. Alcatena's artwork is very appealing, but is maybe a bit cute for this story. The Aliens story that follows is much more memorable, perhaps because the Predator doesn't offer much of a threat to Mega-City One. It kills a lot of people, but it's essentially a nuisance – whereas the Aliens are a plague that threatens total extinction. Henry Flint's art looks a lot like Carlos Ezquerra's, so this feels like authentic Dredd from the beginning. The Mega-City offers a million dark places for an alien to hide and lay its eggs. A space pirate brought them here to conquer the city, but luckily another idiot thought he could breed them for use in fighting pits and got himself infected – his exploding chest and the thing that comes out of him gets Dredd on the case. Great use of Dredd, the Mega-City, and the aliens. *Stephen Theaker* ★★★☆☆

Y: The Last Man, Vol. 4: Safeword, by Brian K. Vaughan, Pia Guerra, Goran Parlov, and José Marzań, Jr (Vertigo)

Yorrick Brown is left alive after a plague killed every other man in the world – and every male creature but one, his monkey Ampersand. In this fourth book, collecting issues 18 to 23 of the original series, he is still travelling across America with Dr Allison Mann and Agent 355. They hope to reach Mann's lab and figure out his immunity, and find a way for the human race to start reproducing again. That's the long-term plan, but right now Ampersand is ailing from the cut he picked up in the previous book. While Agent 355 and Dr Mann go off to get medicine, they leave Yorick with one of 355's retired colleagues, Agent 711. His experiences in her log cabin are eye-opening, to say the least, and we learn that Yorick isn't quite the happy-go-lucky type we had imagined. In the book's second story, "Widow's Pass", the interstate route is blocked by a small but heavily-armed militia, convinced the government is behind the plague and ready to beat any government employees to death until they confess. It's another terrific volume of this series. The story is gripping, both in the day to day events and

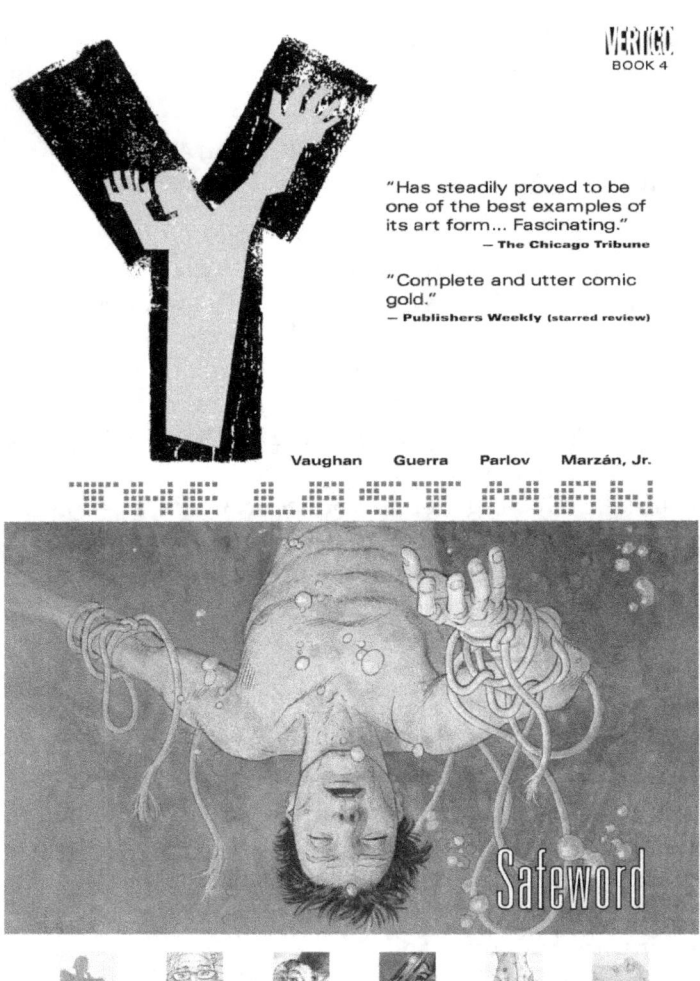

the ongoing mysteries. The artwork and colouring is perfect, the action always totally understandable without giving up any dynamism. And this book gives us many more layers to Yorick's character, as we learn more about his life both before and immediately after the disaster. Best of all is the thoughtful storytelling of the sort that gives us Dr Mann explaining which animal species will die out first, because of their short life cycles: the apocalypse isn't yet over. Very good indeed. *Stephen Theaker* ★★★★☆

Zenith: Phase Two, by Grant Morrison and Steve Yeowell (Rebellion)

Zenith's parents were a couple of superheroes, White Heat and Doctor Beat, murdered in the late sixties. In 1983 he revealed himself to the public, and after becoming popular in the tabloids "he did what all the soap stars and the page three girls were doing". He released a pop record, and then some more, his soaraway success only interrupted by the re-emergence in the previous book of a mad Nazi super-villain. This volume, collecting stories from *2000AD* Progs 589 to 606 and a winter special from 1988, shows us a Zenith who has grown up an infinitesimal amount. He still doesn't want to miss *Neighbours*, he's obsessed with Beatrice Dalle, and he'll hook up with women two at a time in the most dangerous of situations, but he doesn't need all that much convincing to tag along with a CIA operative on her investigation of a Richard Branson type in his mysterious Scottish headquarters. She promises he'll learn something about his family there, and by gum he does. It's great to finally read one of the lost touchstones of 1980s comics. While *V for Vendetta* and *The Dark Knight Returns* are by now in their three millionth and one print runs, this one was unavailable for a fair old while. It's classic Grant

Morrison, its edges overlapping with so much he's done since, from *Doom Patrol* to *The Invisibles* to *Batman*, with its shadowy manipulators, interdimensional invaders and pop culture heroics. Comparing Steve Yeowell's art to that in *The Crimson Seas*, I can see that it's improved over time and become more consistent, but I love it here just as much. Essential reading. *Stephen Theaker* ★★★★☆

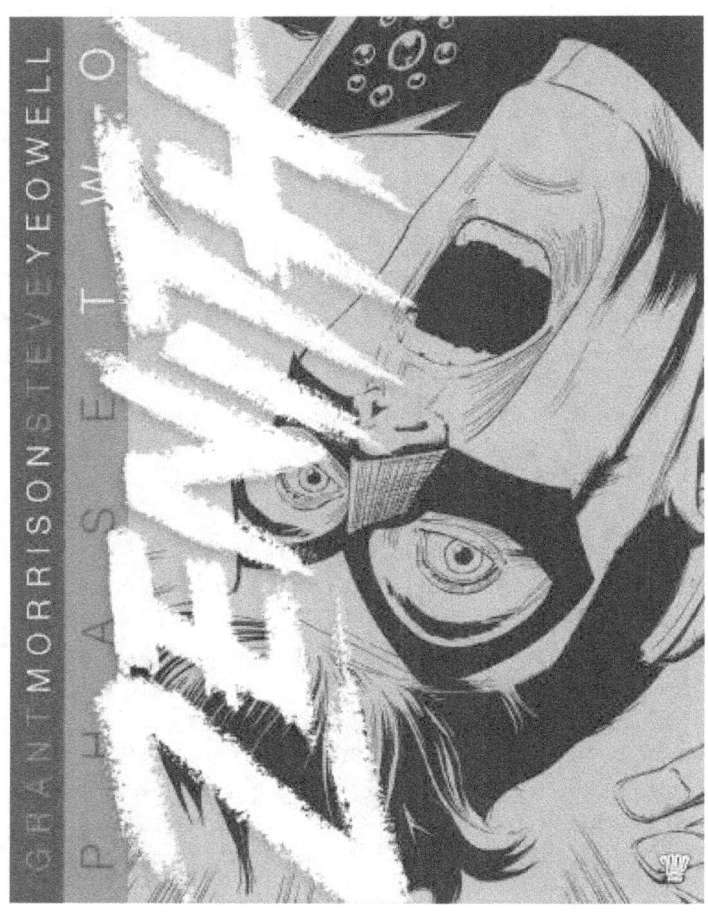

Films

---

10 Cloverfield Lane, by Josh Campbell, Matthew Stuecken and Damien Chazelle (Paramount Pictures et al.)

Character, tension reign in masterwork of claustrophobic uncertainty.

The mind-numbing sameness of many films has trained viewers to expect a narrow list of possibilities as a story unfolds... either *this* will happen or *that* will happen... character X is either all *this* or all *that*. *10 Cloverfield Lane*, directed by Dan Trachtenberg and based loosely on the alien attack extravaganza *Cloverfield* (2008), plays upon this tendency to pigeonhole outcomes and characters. Set mostly in a bunker beneath a Louisiana farm, the film serves up a potent "he's coming/who's out there?" tension gumbo whose ingredients range from bold (and sometimes shocking) actions to more ordinary, yet still highly charged situations.

Aspiring fashion designer Michelle, whose marriage is on the rocks, crashes her car, then wakes up chained to a wall in a kind of cell. Her warden Howard claims that "there's been an attack" and that he's brought her down into his bunker to save her from contaminated air. Michelle then meets farmhand and fellow bunker guest Emmett, who says that Howard also "saved" him from the event. Ex-Navy man Howard gives Michelle a tour of the space that will indefinitely serve as the trio's living quarters.

So begins a play-like film that tangles the viewer in a world of uncertainty controlled by an eccentric doomsday enthusiast (Howard). Michelle, uncertain of her keeper's trustworthiness, enlists Emmett. They gradually uncover more about Howard's mysterious (and absent) daughter Megan while Howard goes to greater lengths to preserve his domain and manage his tenants.

Goodman Leads Great Cast

Interstellar travel and exotic planets dominate the contemporary sci-fi film landscape. *10 Cloverfield Lane* stands apart by confining its activities to a small set

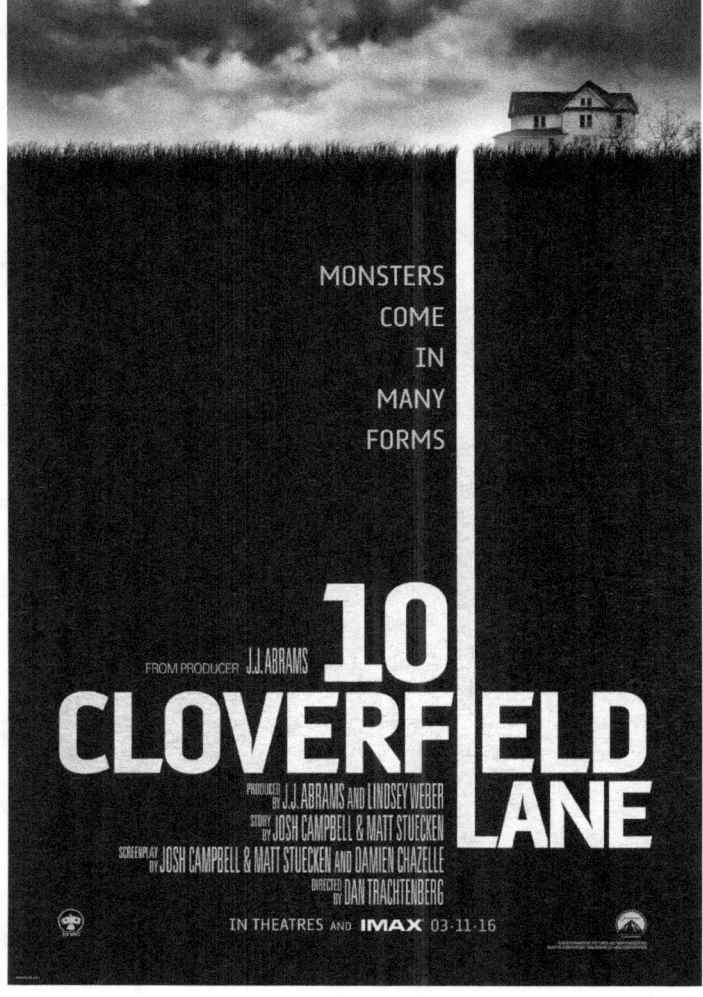

with a bare bones cast of primary characters, all of whom perform superbly.

Mary Elizabeth Winstead's Michelle is a pragmatic young lady: she can devise makeshift weapons and manipulate conversations. Emmett, played by John Gallagher, Jr, serves as a kind of intermediary between Michelle and Howard. Though he first presents as somewhat dim-witted, Emmett quickly proves to be a more thoughtful individual. In one scene, Michelle and Emmett each share a regret story that reveals more about them. By the film's end, both will have an opportunity for redemption.

The most compelling character of *10 Cloverfield Lane* is John Goodman's Howard. From the moment that Howard roughly opens the door and clomps into Michelle's cell, Goodman captivates. You never know what he's going to say or do. He is a commanding figure with little tolerance for horseplay.

Goodman is at his best in scenarios that would typically be seen as ordinary or even banal... eating dinner or playing a game, for instance. When the trio plays a guessing game, Emmett points at Michelle and says, "Michelle is a..." Howard repeats "girl" and grows frustrated as he is unable to come up with the word "woman". In the end, the best Howard can do is "princess". Howard's inability to conceive of Michelle as a woman shows his desire to be a father figure. This fits with the territoriality he expresses toward Michelle throughout the film, such as when he brings her ice cream or chides Emmett ("No touching!") for grabbing Michelle's arm while she stumbles.

A Study in Ambivalence
What makes *10 Cloverfield Lane* such an effective film is its reliance on the viewer's uncertainty. It starts with the trailer: Tommy James and the Shondells' upbeat "I Think We're Alone Now" accompanies warm and fuzzy

scenes like Howard bobbing before his jukebox and the trio playing games. You'd think this was a resurrection of Goodman's Dan Conner from the nineties sitcom *Roseanne*.

But as the trailer and the film prove, 10 Cloverfield Lane is far from the Chicago suburbs where *Roseanne* was set and Howard is nothing like Dan Conner. Howard is not gregarious. He is controlling. He is short-tempered. He is utterly devoid of a sense of humour. Still, we can't help but wonder: is Howard, despite his oddities, correct in his assertions? The questions build: Is Howard lying? Is he crazy? Is the air contaminated? Are we "alone now?" One isn't even certain that Emmett can be trusted.

Then there are the bigger concerns: Will Michelle get out? And what happens if she does?

The tenuous connection to the film *Cloverfield* is another master stroke of ambiguity. For instance, the occasional rumblings the group hears above the bunker could be aliens (like *Cloverfield*), or they could be a misdirection... cars, helicopters, maybe even something that Howard manufactured.

Strange Creatures

To see 10 Cloverfield Lane in a theatre or even in a dark room is to descend alongside Michelle into Howard's shelter. During your journey, you'll crawl through confined spaces, and you'll participate in escape attempts both subtle and blatant.

"People are strange creatures," says Howard. "You can't always convince them that safety is in their best interest." On Howard's turf, you can never be safe in your assumptions about just what is going on.

Can this film, which boldly refuses to conform to Hollywood tropes, even be classified as sci-fi? There's only one place to go to find out: 10 Cloverfield Lane. *Douglas J. Ogurek* ★★★★★

The Boy, by Stacey Menear (Huayi Brothers Pictures et al.)

Just when you thought the creepy doll approach had run its course, along comes Brahms.

Years ago, Mr Heelshire, having imbibed one too many spirits, described his long-deceased son Brahms with a single word: "odd". Such is the tone that characterizes *The Boy*, a film about a doll that may or may not embody the spirit of its namesake, who died in a fire at age eight.

Though it hit theatres in January, a month notorious for horror duds, *The Boy* is good. It's better than good. Directed by William Brent Bell, the film offers a creepy antagonist and some genuinely freaky experiences. It's less about jump scares – there are a few – and more about lingering unease.

Gretta Evans, fleeing an abusive ex-boyfriend back in the States, takes on a live-in nanny job at an English manor. It isn't long before the property's elderly owners (the Heelshires) reveal that their beloved son Brahms is a porcelain doll.

"If you're good to Brahms, he'll be good to you," says Mr Heelshire. "If you're bad—" Mrs Heelshire doesn't let her husband finish. So the couple takes off, but not before the missus whispers to Gretta, "I'm so sorry." Thanks for the vote of confidence!

Gretta, equipped only with her own scepticism and a list of "rules" ranging from "Never leave Brahms alone" to "Kiss goodnight", throws a blanket over Brahms and calls it a day. She soon learns that something is definitely up with that doll.

Brahms's antics begin with subtle mischief and gradually escalate, while Gretta's human interactions are limited to calls with a friend back home and the occasional exchange with love interest Malcolm, the Heelshires' "grocery boy".

Is He Alive, or Isn't He?
Doll antagonists like to go berserk. Think Chucky, or
the even more extreme tribal doll from *Trilogy of
Terror* (1975). Brahms, on the other hand, takes the
opposite approach: he remains motionless. It's when
you can't see him that Brahms does his thing. Thus, he
achieves a much higher level of menace than his
dynamic counterparts.

The Boy casts its spell by keeping us on the fence. Is Brahms endowed with supernatural powers? Or is he some elaborate hoax?

Then there's the doll's appearance. Brahms isn't ugly, nor is he done up in vivid colours. Rather, with his pale complexion and deep brown eyes, Brahms represents the over-protected, shy schoolboy. He is proper... fragile even. He might also be champing at the bit to cause some mischief.

Often the camera lingers on the doll's face to bring discomfort to the viewer. Is that thing going to blink? Will it move its little arm?

A Little Dickens

The Boy starts slow, lulling the viewer into a tea and biscuits (with some red herring) atmosphere. It reminds me of the quiet films that supported my high school and early college readings of nineteenth century British literature. There's the manor with its classical architecture and ornate interior woodwork. There's the garden and the statuary.

However, Brahms Heelshire plays a much different tune than the Brahms (Johannes) that was Dickens's contemporary.

Whether the filmgoer approaches it with a "figure it out" or an "in the moment" mentality, *The Boy* offers an experience as memorable and unsettling as the "tink tink" of a finger tapping porcelain. *Douglas J. Ogurek* ★★★★☆

Deadpool, by Rhett Reese and Paul Wernick (Fox)

Sorry Iron Man: you're no longer the most entertaining superhero.

We expect a couple of things from a good superhero movie. First, of course, is action punctuated by violence. We're happy if we walk away with a favourite scene or two. Second is a superhero who's fun to watch. If we're lucky, he or she will charm us with a couple of quotable quotes.

Choosing such scenes or quotes for *Deadpool*, directed by Tim Miller, proves problematic. That's because *every* scene entertains... and almost everything this film's namesake says (and he says a lot) elicits at least a chuckle.

Typically, people who don't stop talking annoy us. Ryan Reynolds's Wade Wilson/Deadpool talks... and talks... and talks. He never stops. But here's the difference: whether he's skipping, getting tortured, taking a cab ride, or hacking off bad guys' (or his own) limbs, this audience addressing antihero leaves the viewer wanting more.

There's something awfully compelling about a protagonist who pops his head out of a mid-air, upside-down vehicle and says, "Shit. Did I leave the stove on?"

Deadpool, which broke the box office record for an R-rated film's opening weekend, shows keen awareness of its position in a long line of superhero films, and it exploits that position brilliantly.

Typical Superhero Story, Atypical Storytelling Techniques

What Wade Wilson wants is pretty straightforward: to apprehend Francis/Ajax, the villain responsible for Wilson's Freddy Krueger-like complexion. It's the way the story unfolds, however, where *Deadpool* makes its mark.

As soon as the opening credits roll, the film sets itself apart: instead of stars' names, superhero film character tropes (e.g. "the hot chick", "the British villain", "a moody teen") and other gems appear.

The story begins with a day in the life of Deadpool. A super-extended action sequence (with references to everything from Monty Python and Judy Blume to *127*

Hours) periodically flashes back to how Wilson obtained his powers. Such storytelling acrobatics echo Deadpool's thrillingly unnecessary spinning flips. Moreover, plunging the viewer into the action underscores the potency of this character.

Then, down comes the fourth wall, which Deadpool not only breaks, but obliterates with Ferris Buelleresque panache. Wilson plays off superhero film clichés while boldly conceding his own role as a character in a movie. He preps us for another character's "superhero landing". He stops the music that accompanies the overused slow-mo superhero walk so he can make a phone call. He speculates on whether the conspicuous underpopulation of the X-Men headquarters that he visits stems from his film's budgetary restrictions.

In the ultimate fourth wall mischief, Deadpool pokes fun at Ryan Reynolds the actor's looks-rather-than-acting-fuelled rise and at Reynolds's disastrous *Green Lantern* (2011) movie. He even comments on "breaking a fourth wall within a fourth wall".

A Stark Departure
The Marvel cinematic superhero roster, despite its continuing success, stood to benefit from another eccentric character. Yes, the Avengers films are highly enjoyable, but doesn't all that teamwork slightly detract from the narcissistic splendour of Tony Stark/Iron Man?

Along comes *Deadpool*, shrewdly marketed as the (wink wink) perfect date movie (which doesn't escape Wilson's commentary) for Valentine's Day weekend. And couples do get a love story of sorts, but more important, they get a new kind of superhero whose moxie transcends that of Iron Man.

Undoubtedly Robert Downey Jr's Tony Stark/Iron Man did a lot for the superhero subgenre, but

Reynolds's Wilson, with his chummy approach, contemporary cultural references, rebellion against superhero conventions, and crude asides better connects with adult viewers.

Examples? Okay. Iron Man flies around in a computerized metal suit that is the result of his engineering genius. Deadpool takes the cab (and doesn't pay the driver). Iron Man has an arsenal

embedded in his suit. Deadpool throws his weapons in a Hello Kitty bag, which he's prone to forget. Tony Stark lives in a beautiful cliff-side contemporary home surrounded by his inventions. Wade Wilson rooms with an elderly blind woman in a cluttered apartment. He passes gas as he walks by her and says, "Hashtag drive-by." Stark wouldn't do that.

Tony "It's moments like these when I realise how much of a superhero I am" Stark is a narcissist. Wade "This shit's gonna have nuts in it" Wilson is a smart-ass. Who would *you* rather spend time with? *Douglas J. Ogurek* ★★★★★

Gods of Egypt, by Matt Sazama and Burk Sharpless (Pyramania et al.)

Dumb. One-dimensional. Loved it.

If you like epic fantasy action films that seem conceived by seventh grade boys, then *Gods of Egypt* is for you. "Look, Johnny: you can remove the smartest god's brain and it's blue. It sparkles too. Then you can put it in your own head and you get smarter!"

The film wrings some of the residual cool from the ultra-violent and ultra-stylish *300* (2006)... even going so far as to reinvent that film's star (Gerard Butler) as chief antagonist/bad boy god Set.

When you watch *Gods of Egypt*, directed by Alex Proyas, just let your brain go and indulge in a dumbed down smorgasbord of everything you need to tantalise the twelve-year-old boy within: fights, acrobatics, shapeshifting, death traps, weapons, cleavage, capes, armour, and, most important, *monsters*!

It even offers a He-Man cartoon style beat-you-over-the-head moral that what you do in this life matters... that good deeds and compassion trump power and vengeance.

The time is "before history began", when Egyptian

gods walked among their devotees. And how do we tell god from mortal? Easy: gods are twice the size of humans, of course!

Horus (Nikolaj Coster-Waldau), god of the sky and son of the beloved Osiris, spends his days partying with the goddess of love Hathor (Elodie Yung). Just as Horus is about to assume the crown, uncle Set (Butler), equipped with a lust for power and a Scottish

accent, transforms into a metallic-looking animal, tears out Horus's eyes (which become blue jewels), and then usurps the throne.

Horus loses his ability to fly and goes into hiding, but all is not lost: young human Bek plans to brave a booby-trapped path to steal back Horus's eyes (at least one of them), then convince the god to defeat Set and assume his rightful position. Thus god (now sporting an eye patch) and human embark on a journey during which Horus's ultimate objective will waver between vengeance and compassion.

In the meantime, the impulsive Set, exuding that Butlerian machismo, does all the things a twelve-year-old boy would do. He builds a towering monument to his space-dwelling father Ra. He gets mad enough to chop off his own soldier's head. He oppresses his people. His lust for power grows. "I cannot be fulfilled," he tells his estranged wife Nepthys. Set even changes the admissions price to the afterworld: before it was good deeds; now it's treasure.

In the film's best scene, two gigantic fire-breathing snakes mounted by goddesses with serpent tongues – do you see the connection there? – pursue Horus and Bek. When the snakes first approach, one chooses to crash through some ruins when it could easily have gone around them. Destruction for destruction's sake. Yay!

There are moments in the film that are quite humorous, particularly when the gods lose their cool. For instance, when Bek urges Horus to run faster during the snake pursuit, the god responds worriedly, "I can't!" Even better: when Anubis discovers his underworld is under threat, the hitherto collected and eloquent god of death breaks into an "oh no!" performance that would make Scooby Doo proud.

Thankfully, the gods of Egypt aren't above one liners. In the midst of battle, one enemy reminds

Horus that he can no longer fly. "Neither can you," he responds. You can guess the rest.

The juvenile way that the gods are portrayed also evokes a chuckle. For instance, when Horus visits his grandfather Ra's solar ship (in outer space), we get a three minute reprieve during which Ra engages in his daily ritual of keeping a space-dwelling demon from destroying the earth. Here we have a top tier actor (Geoffrey Rush), wide-eyed and engulfed in digital flames, using a staff to shoot flame bursts at the gigantic creature.

But perhaps no god embodies the seventh grade mentality as well as Thoth, god of wisdom. To underscore his deep contemplations, he holds his hands behind his back and sometimes even holds a fist beneath his chin á la Rodin's *The Thinker*. At one point, Thoth holds a bunch of leaf lettuce and mulls over "its essence, its mystery, its truth". Horus rips it away and says, "It's lettuce!"

So follow Horus's example: don't approach *Gods of Egypt* wearing your critic's hat or seeking wisdom; just enjoy the crunchiness of a good action film. *Douglas J. Ogurek* ★★★★☆

The Witch, by Robert Eggers (Parts and Labor et al.)

Fellow horror fans: we've been duped!

The critic endorsements that decorate the trailer for *The Witch* would have us believe that this film, written and directed by Robert Eggers, would scare the pants off us. "One of the most genuinely unnerving horror films in recent memory," says one. "Will make your blood run cold," cautions another. That's verbal candy for the horror aficionado.

For months, I anticipated the jitters that films like *The Blair Witch Project* (1999), *The Ring* (2002) and *Paranormal Activity* (2007) heaped upon me.

There was, however, a bit of trepidation about that preview: the excerpts that accompanied those tasty quotes didn't show anything especially groundbreaking. That observation turned out to be telling.

As *The Witch* progressed, I kept asking myself, "When's this going to start getting frightening?" Sadly, at some point, I realised it just wasn't going to happen. *The Witch* fails to deliver as a horror film. Moreover,

those few scenes that led to its (mis)categorisation as a horror are clichés, some of which are laughable.

The film does offer strong acting, period authenticity, and cinematography that reflects the self-suppression and bleakness that characterized Puritan New England. But that's not why I came to see this film. I came because I wanted to poop my pants in fear.

A Banished Family Falling Apart
William, Katherine, and their five children get banished from their plantation for religious differences, then set out to live on their own. "We will conquer this wilderness," says William (played by Ralph Ineson, whose voice is as gritty as a Puritan wardrobe). "It will not consume us."

Then baby Sam's disappearance triggers intensifying familial strife, the brunt of which gets directed toward oldest child Thomasin. She's accused of being a witch by supremely annoying toddler twins Jonas and Mercy. Mother Katherine accuses her of stealing an heirloom. Characters argue, then pray. They chastise each other, then go into the woods. They point fingers, then berate themselves.

Underpinning and fuelling all of this is the threat of a witch (or witches) that inhabit the forest. Ee hee hee hee!

A Sheep in Goat's Clothing
If you're into period pieces about one of the grimmest eras in American history, then you'll have a blast... maybe that's not the right word. *The Witch* captures the harshness of the time, the perils of religious extremism, and the subjugation of devotees (especially women). The film's focus on authenticity leads to the dialogue's heavy accents and unfamiliar diction – Ineson's gravelly voice doesn't help – that made it a bit

difficult for a (American) Midwesterner like me to understand.

Again, achieving historical accuracy wasn't the film's conveyed purpose; generating fear was. Thus, *The Witch* is a historical drama touted as a horror even though there are only a couple *somewhat* frightening scenes slapped onto it. Perhaps the most unnerving aspect of the film is the discordant, high-pitched chorus that accompanies views of the forest's edge.

Not All That Doesn't Glitter...
So where's all this critical acclaim coming from? Clearly the endless onslaught of one-dimensional action films irks critics, but have they become so jaded that for them, anything with extended shots, sparse sets, and economy of movement warrants a triumph?

Last year, they got it right for *It Follows*, an understated film that *was* conceptually innovative and *did* provoke fear. That film offered a brilliant ending with thematically sensitive camerawork and an alarmingly abrupt final cut. Conversely, the concluding scene of *The Witch* is silly. Plus, I've seen that. I've read that.

Maybe the critics believe *The Witch* makes some statement about the suppression of women. I don't care. It didn't entertain me enough to put thought into that theme. I wanted a horror film and they lied to me. The repression of women isn't frightening. It just sucks.

Perhaps one filmgoer's parting comment best encapsulates the typical person's response to *The Witch*: "That wasn't really frightening. Just depressing."

Don't be fooled by the critics' assertions of a "slow build". A slow build to what? I was looking for a skyscraper; what I got was a Lego block. *Douglas J. Ogurek* ★★★☆☆

Games

Fallout 4 (PS4) by Bethesda Softworks (Bethesda)

I didn't mention this in the editorial, but Bethesda are partly responsible for a huge distraction when it came to putting this issue together. Having bought a PS4 with *Fallout 4* as part of the package, and being a bit of a *Fallout 3* and *Fallout New Vegas* vet, I was eager to load the game, having watched various YouTube first playthrough and guide vids. Time exists as an entirely different entity when playing this game, as your perception of the outside world is taken over by this new reality. Crazy!

The game is an *astonishing* achievement, certainly a leap far beyond that of *Fallout 3* and the latter *Fallout New Vegas*. Obviously the visual and audio aspects are superior due to the PS4's processors, but Bethesda have built upon the unique gaming concept of the previous Fallout offerings and improved upon the idea superbly. Not that *Fallout 4* is without its minor faults – but these can be excused as the game is just *so* damn good, and looks absolutely beautiful. Reading back through this review, I can honestly say that I'm only scratching the surface of the whole experience – to go into *great* depth would be impossible within these pages, and any attempt by me to do so would only serve to spoil the game. I'm just gonna stick to some of the core aspects, just to give you a flavour.

The backstory is simple: In a 1950sesque U.S. / future alternate history mashup, atomic war begins. You run with your family to a Vault where you will be protected from the devastation. You awake early to witness your (in my case) wife being killed in her hypersleep chamber and your infant son kidnapped. Escaping the vault to track down your son, you are greeted by an atomic wasteland. Various mutated beasts and creatures inhabit this wasteland, and as the story unfolds you – as per previous Fallout outings into the wasteland – establish yourself with the many and varied inhabitants and factions you encounter. There's a great depth here. The game's narrative provides a convincing array of human and non-human groups and settlements, all with their own unique take on life in the wasteland. It's easy to get caught up in the dialog of these characters – where before with *Fallout 3*, I found myself skipping a lot of the dialog and interactive conversation choices to just get on with it. With 4, I find myself listening more, taking in all the information, interacting more with the characters. This is down not only to the visuals, but also the voice

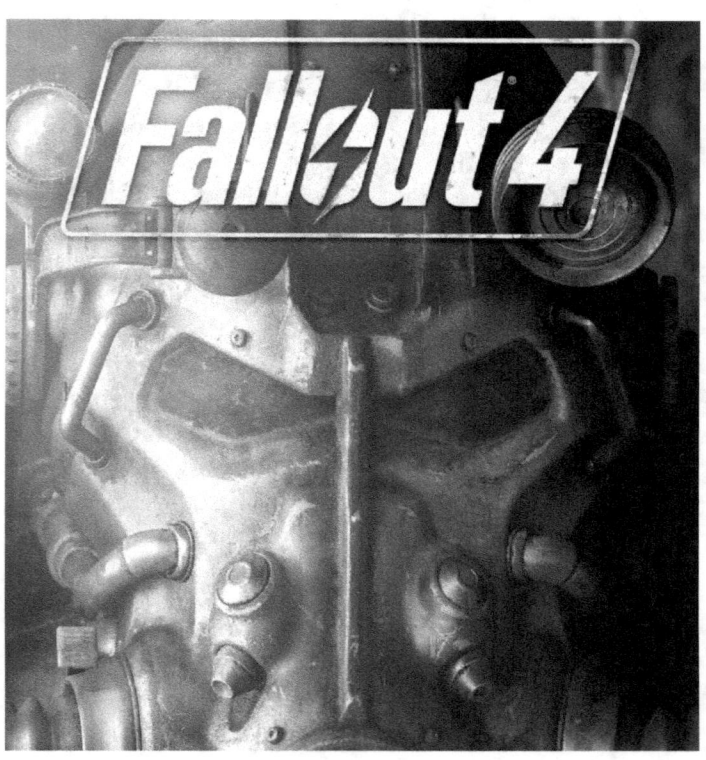

acting. There's a lot of info dumping here, but it all knits together to form this vast tapestry which is the wasteland. Bethesda have removed the You're good for doing / saying this / that, you're bad for doing / saying this / that / idea which could instantly stall the game as you hit pause to consider the ramifications of your actions. New Vegas suffered from being bogged down with *so* many choices of which character or group to befriend, it became a real problem, taking away from the enjoyment of actually moving around the environment and, well, playing. Saying this, *Fallout 4* is hardly a "game" as such – it's more of a simulation. You're out there in the wilderness, trying to find your son, trying to stay alive. On the way you'll be offered companionship, but I chose to stick with my first companion offering, an Alsatian called Dogmeat. He helps you through tough spots, sniffs gear out for you to pick up, and provides a few lighter moments as he rolls around in the dirt, or finds a teddy bear to play with. All this love for a digital dog, from a cat man!

This survival concept is but a small part of the whole. As before with Bethesda's *Skyrim*, you can craft weapons, harvest food to cook potions for healing and power-ups. But the experience is far more than just that. Now you can build settlements, encourage settlers to be part of your community, but hey – if you don't provide basics such as food, water, shelter, electricity, defence, a bed to sleep in and a roof over their heads, they get grumpy. This is where the "game" really sets itself apart. Suddenly you the participant have changed the pace. You can ignore a mission asking you to defend another farm or plant nursery from rampaging raiders, and build, slow the game down and enjoy the addictive pleasure of constructing a community and looking after these poor souls that have chosen to join you, and at your pace. Shacks, small houses, animal pens, bridge walkways, fenced off gardens can be built to name a few. This is where the "game" sets itself above others, as practically every item in the wasteland has a value – not only monetary, but also (and more importantly for this aspect) as a material commodity. Steel, plastic, wood, oil, glass, electronics, you name it, they can all be scavenged and stored to be utilised to build your settlement. These materials can also be used to upgrade weapons and power armour. Once a settlement thrives, you can move on to another, help them, plant more food to attract more settlers and then set up trade routes between them to provide income for yourself. It's a bonkers concept, but one we can all identify with. No player settlement will be identical to another's. My daughter decided for her game, the most important aspect of her settlement are small "personal" shacks with just two beds, rather than my large dormitory building holding 17 beds. Opposite her curved metal bedrooms she built toilets, replete with "his" and "hers" signs, and if I know her, to follow will probably be a bloody great white picket fenced garden, growing corn, potatoes, melons, gourds, defended by a couple of machine gun turrets.

If this all sounds a little too twee, then the options are there to just go out and explore and pick up missions to up your XP and level up. Set a marker on your map and you'll come across beautiful vistas of devastation. Towns and cities you cannot refuse to explore, as exploration's in our nature. And in these highly detailed locations, when the sun's going down and the rain courses through the streets, lightning momentarily illuminating the damp bricks and rusted cars as the thunder booms, you'll round a corner and find...

Well, absolutely anything really. It's up to you to find out.

Recommended. Howard Watts

Television

Ash vs Evil Dead, by Ivan Raimi and chums (Starz/Virgin Media)

Ash Williams is a sexist jerk with an unfortunate tendency to unleash the forces of hell upon the world. Thirty years ago he found a *Necronomicon* while on a trip to a cabin in the woods with his girlfriend, and ended up having to squash her head in a vice and cut off his own hand with a chainsaw. Neither has forgiven him. As this ten-part series starts, the Deadites have

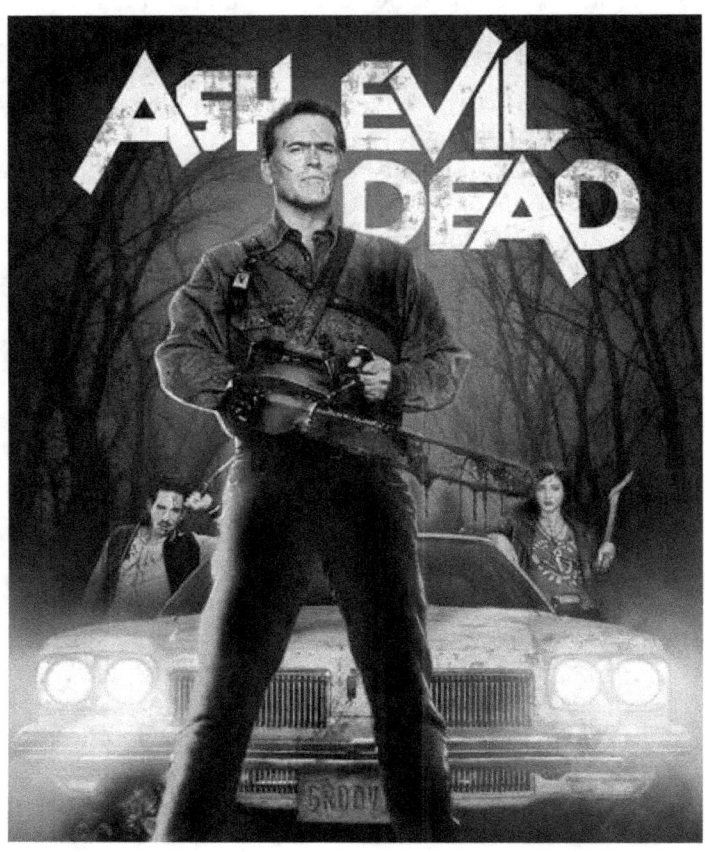

been quiet for a while, but he still keeps a boomstick in his mobile home. It proves handy after the idiot gets high with a sozzled friend and reads from his *Necronomicon*... The evil dead return in force, and so Ash, reluctantly, gathers friends to help in the fight. It's all a bit daft – the spirits seem to be able to take over anybody whenever they like, so the only reason Ash survives is presumably because they like playing with him – but it doesn't quite reach the stark raving lunacy of *Evil Dead II*. There are lots of good jump scares, some excellent monsters and one-liners, and it is refreshingly gory. The half hour format works well for the show – it would be hard to keep up the intensity for an hour. Ash's boorishness and the misogyny of the language used when female characters are possessed is partly balanced by a diverse cast. Ash develops an appealing relationship with Special Agent Fisher, an African-American cop who seems to like him for the idiot that he is, and the scenes with his two likeable protégés are always watchable – they're a bit like the Doctor, Rory and Amy, if the Doctor were a buffoon and Rory worshipped him anyway. *Stephen Theaker* ★★★☆☆

Fear the Walking Dead, Season 1, by Robert Kirkman and chums (AMC)

Travis Manawa (played by Cliff Curtis) and Madison Clark (Kim Dickens) are a married couple trying without much luck to blend a family. He is divorced, she is a widow. Travis has a son who lives with his ex and doesn't want to see him at the weekends, Madison has a son, Nicky, who loves heroin and a daughter, Alicia, who hates long trousers. When Nicky wakes up in a drug den to find his girlfriend eating someone's face, he thinks he's gone mad, and so does his family, but it won't be long before everyone is caught up in

that madness. When a riot breaks out in the city centre, Travis and his son take refuge in a hairdressers with a family of three, emigrants from El Salvador, not realising that from now on, all refuge will be temporary.

American television has a lamentable tendency to suck the vitality out of any successful television programme by creating licensed rip-offs and copycats. For every worthwhile *Xena* or *Angel* there are a dozen *NCISes: LA* or *CSIs: New York* that overstretch the premise or divide the writing staff. *Fear the Walking Dead* spins out of a programme that itself has sometimes been spread a little thin, despite its quality, having to ration the appearances of some cast members. But this spin-off has one big selling point: where the usual colonates just show us slightly different people doing a slightly different job under a slightly different colour filter, *Fear the Walking Dead* can show us a crucial part of its parent's story, one that viewers missed while Rick Grimes was sleeping in hospital: how the apocalypse went down. Part of the reason we didn't see that before was that it had been shown in so many films, so why repeat it? Get to the stuff we don't know! But that world means more to us now. We know how bad it is going to get for these people, we shout at the screen as they waste batteries, and cringe at their pitifully small fences!

As slowly becomes clear, there is another difference: while the characters on *The Walking Dead* have generally made the right decisions, have usually been the good guys, these people aren't. They aren't the kind of people who think to close the door behind them after they escape a zombie hideout, not all of them would rush out to warn people in danger, and some of them don't care about the consequences of their actions at all. This first season is only six episodes long, and while the first couple are more about junkies

and family drama than the undead, it gets better as it goes on, and from the beginning it has a undeniable heft, borrowed from its parent show, admittedly, but very real nevertheless. It doesn't yet have a central performance to match Andrew Lincoln's in *The Walking Dead*, but neither do any other programmes, and these characters haven't yet been stripped so raw as Rick Grimes. It will come. *Stephen Theaker*
★★★☆☆

Jessica Jones, Season 1, by Melissa Rosenberg and chums (Marvel/Netflix)

Jessica Jones is a private eye, and she's down on her luck, doing jobs for a shady lawyer that don't always bring out her best side. Traumatised by having fallen under the mental control of a powerful psychic for a long period, and the things he forced her to do during that time, she's drinking too much and not looking after herself. She has a couple of things going for her: superstrength (though no more invulnerability than is required to punch people very hard without breaking your own arm) and a good friend, former child star Patsy Walker. (Their friendship and its history is one of my favourite things about the programme.) Sadly, we're not joining Jessica at the point where things start to pick up for her. She does meet a new guy, Luke Cage, who seems able to deal with the worst drunks in Hell's Kitchen without taking a scratch, but it's not one of those relationships built on mutual trust, at least at first. And she's beginning to think that Kilgrave, her psychic tormentor, might be back, and it's impossible to make anyone believe her when he can just order people to forget that they've ever seen him. He is back (and played with a gleefully childish lack of conscience by David Tennant), and he's going

to cause a lot of trouble before the thirteen-episode series is over.

Jessica is played by Krysten Ritter, from *Don't Trust the B– in Apartment 23* and *Veronica Mars* (fans of that show may also enjoy this darker take on the same genre). It's not the most obvious casting, since she's best known for comedy, but she's very good, conveying all the moods and troubles of her character perfectly.

Everyone in the programme is equally well cast, and it's well directed, and always interesting. Overall, I enjoyed it, but it drove me up the wall, the longer it went on. Some people might see the problems I had with it as nitpicking, but to me they were fundamental flaws. Jessica and her friends are trying to defeat an enemy who can order anyone to follow his instructions, but they don't use earplugs, they don't wear noise-cancelling headphones, they don't do any of the perfectly obvious things you would do to cope with someone who has those powers. And they can't convince anyone to believe he has powers, even though SHIELD, at the very least, know of an Asgardian with the same gimmick, and everyone would know about the superpowers of Thor and the Hulk. It might have been better if Kilgrave and his powers had been brought to the fore a bit later in the series, coming in for the finale rather than being the main antagonist for the whole thing, because, much as I like David Tennant and love his portrayal of this repellent character, his powers don't stand up to twelve hours of scrutiny – even if the show does find interesting ways to use them. I'm looking forward to season two, though. *Stephen Theaker* ★★★☆☆

Sherlock: The Abominable Bride, by Mark Gatiss and Steven Moffat (2entertain Ltd)

Theaker's Quarterly Fiction may seem an unlikely venue for a review of the first full-length *Sherlock* special, shown on all small screens and some big screens across the UK on New Year's Day 2016. Three mini-seasons (of three episodes each) and one mini-special (of just over seven minutes) in, however, the world of *Sherlock* is already brim-full of superhuman beings. The eponymous protagonist refers to himself as "a high-functioning sociopath" (one of the series' most-repeated phrases, suggesting sociopaths are usually low-functioning), but his superpowers include: reading an entire life history in a glance, disarming sword-wielding assassins without breaking a sweat, destroying international crime syndicates single-handedly, successfully masquerading as an extremist in Karachi, riding a motorbike safely at breakneck speed, instantly recovering from consuming vast quantities of Class A drugs... and returning from the dead. His nemesis, supervillain Moriarty, has his own list of powers: controlling Cockney serial killers, Chinese secret societies, and Eastern European paramilitaries; breaking into the Tower of London, the Bank of England, and Pentonville Prison simultaneously; resisting "enhanced interrogation" indefinitely... and returning from the dead (which is what the special is all about). Even Mycroft, whose powers are intellectual rather than physical, can follow his brother's clandestine footsteps across Europe, masquerade as a Serbian soldier without detection, and take charge of a Tactical Firearms Command team. In fact, poor old Watson is the foil to at least four superhumans as "His Last Vow" (season 3, episode 3) reveals that Mrs Watson is a (semi-retired) super-villain-turned-hero, able to fire a handgun with one hundred percent accuracy, pass through multiple layers of physical security without trace, evade the joint efforts of NATO's intelligence services, instantly access information beyond the combined capacity of MI5, MI6, and GCHQ... and waltz in a wedding dress. All of which to say that the BBC's *Sherlock* is very much a mix of genres, alternating between detective stories in an urban fantasy setting and high fantasy in a tragic clash of good and evil – not to mention regular dashes of comedy.

The mix of crime and speculative fiction is by no means a flaw (though I hope to have conveyed a mildly disapproving tone) and may well account for the show's popularity – along with the star qualities Benedict Cumberbatch, Martin Freeman, and Andrew Scott (recently Bond villain Max Denbigh in *Spectre*) bring to the small screen. The generic motley also serves, conveniently, to distinguish *Sherlock* from *Elementary*, CBS's contemporary Holmes series, which is pure crime fiction and currently in its fourth season (of twenty-four episodes each). Given the template of

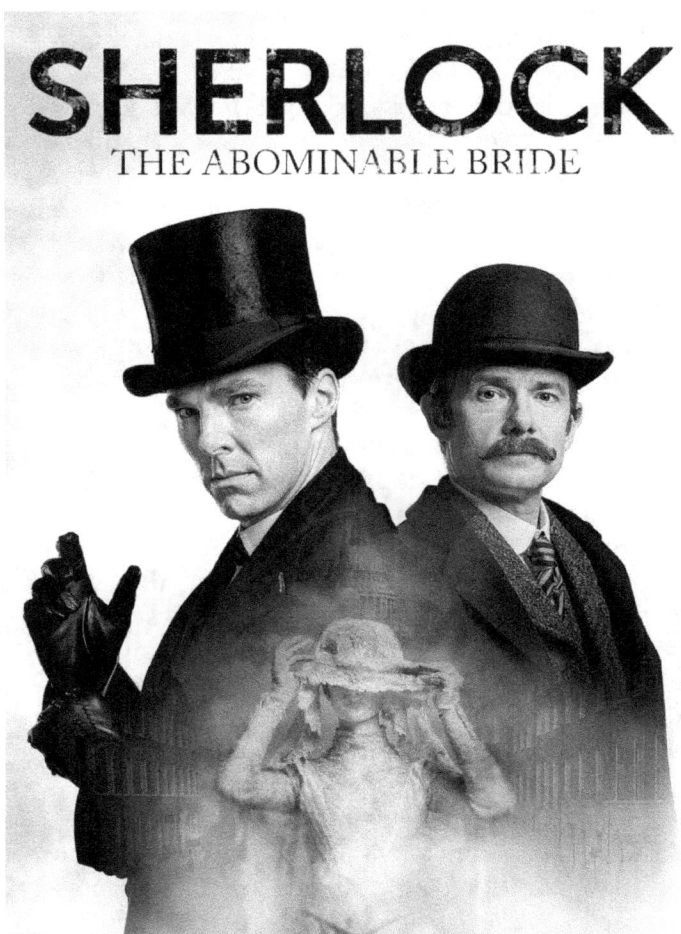

detective-story-within-urban-fantasy, *The Abominable
Bride* is exemplary, with murder mystery and high
fantasy prised apart for most of the episode. Prior to
the original screening, much was made of
Cumberbatch and Freeman appearing in Victorian
garb, suggesting that the special would be outside the
overarching narrative of the series, but the first few
seconds drop this pretence and story picks up precisely
where "His Last Vow" finished. Minutes after Holmes'
departure into exile (and certain death) for the murder
of Charles Augustus Magnussen (a particularly nasty
villain), Moriarty's face appears on all the television
screens across the country asking, "Did you miss me?"
Holmes is recalled, the plane turns around... and we
appear to go back in time to 1895. *The* (Case of the)
Abominable Bride takes its title from Conan Doyle's
"The Musgrave Ritual", where Holmes mentions
"Ricoletti of the club-foot, and his abominable wife" as
a case he investigated prior to meeting Watson. Doyle
was fond of making these references to unpublished
cases in order to give the impression that Holmes had
a life beyond the printed page and they are scattered
throughout the original short stories and novellas.
Theaker's Quarterly Fiction contributor John Hall
(whose stories from issues 23 to 29 were collected in
Five Forgotten Stories, published by Theaker's
Paperback Library in 2011) analysed them all in *The
Abominable Wife and Other Unrecorded Cases of Mr
Sherlock Holmes* (Calabash Press, 1998). Drawing
attention to the fact that Doyle either let his
imagination run away with him or was flexing his
sense of humour – aside from abominable wives, there
are remarkable worms, trained cormorants, red
leeches, and flying false teeth – John takes
"abominable wife" as a metaphor for all the references.
The abominable wife serves a similar supplementary
purpose in *Sherlock*, the idea being that if Holmes can

solve the 1895 case he can work out the 2014 case of Moriarty's resurrection.

Back in 1895, Emelia Ricoletti (made up to resemble Heath Ledger's Joker from *The Dark Knight* in an already over-used trope) fires two six-shooters into a crowded London street from her balcony before blowing her brains out. Her body is removed to the morgue, but that evening she conspicuously gives her husband both barrels of a shotgun in front of a police constable. Holmes, Watson, and a shaken Lestrade arrive at the morgue to find that Mrs Ricoletti's corpse appears to have written "You" on the wall in blood after the murder of her husband. Holmes doesn't get very far with the investigation, but a few months later Lady Carmichael hires him to protect her husband from Mrs Ricoletti, whose ghost has been seen walking in the grounds of their estate. Holmes and Watson fail to save Lord Carmichael, giving them two murders to solve. By two-thirds of the way through *The Abominable Bride*, it becomes clear that the Victorian case is taking place in Holmes' "mind palace" (where he retrieves information from his near-eidetic memory) and that he is fixating on the (very) cold Ricoletti case because he thinks Moriarty has used the same method to fake his own death in "The Reichenbach Fall" (season 2, episode 3). The solution to the 1895 case is rather disappointing and I disclose no spoilers when I say that Mrs Ricoletti was indeed dead by the time of the second murder (where she was not positively identified), but not the first (where she was). This suggests that Moriarty is actually dead. Holmes shouts "There are no ghosts!" in 1895 and confirms "Moriarty is dead, no question" in 2014, but there are plenty of questions left unanswered, not to mention some ambiguity, at the conclusion of the 2014 case. If Moriarty is indeed dead, then *The Abominable Bride* is a giant red herring in much the same way as

John characterises all of Doyle's teasers (the references as abominable wives to the admirable husbands of the published stories). More likely it is just that, a teaser of suitable ambiguity aimed at whetting audience appetites for season 4. Unfortunately for fans, filming hasn't yet begun and Sherlock won't be on screens until 2017 at the earliest. In the interim, I recommend *Elementary* for a gritty and realistic contemporary take on the Great Detective. *The Abominable Bride* DVD contains two discs and if, like me, you are not enticed by the prospect of "over an hour of Bonus Features" there is always the double-sided poster to colour in (advertising *Sherlock: The Mind Palace*, published by BBC Books last year). *Rafe McGregor*

Notes

Also Received, But Not Yet Reviewed
Notes by Stephen Theaker

Gumeny, Eirik, *Revenge-aroni* (Jersey Devil Press)
Lovegrove, James, *World of Water* (Rebellion): really
    enjoyed *World of Fire*, and this follow-up was great
    fun too – review planned for *Interzone* #265.
Simsa, Cyril, *Lost Cartographies* (Invocations Press)
Suddain, M., *Hunters & Collectors* (Jonathan Cape)
Weisman, Jacob (ed.), *Invaders* (Tachyon
    Publications): science fiction stories by writers
    from outside the sf genre.
Westley, Michael, *Thimblestar* (Immanion Press)
Whiteley, Aliya, *The Arrival of Missives* (Unsung
    Stories)

About TQF

Copyright

ISBN (print): 978-1-910387-15-3
ISBN (epub): 978-1-910387-16-0

ISSN (print): 1747-6083
ISSN (online): 1747-6075

Website: www.theakersquarterly.blogspot.com

Email: theakersquarterlyfiction@gmail.com

Lulu Store: www.lulu.com/silveragebooks

Feedbooks: www.feedbooks.com/userbooks/tag/tqf

Submissions: Submissions are very welcome! See website for guidelines and terms.

Advertising: We welcome ad swaps with small press publishers and other creative types, and we'll run ads for relevant new projects from former contributors.

Sending material for review: We are interested in reviewing almost anything that's fantasy-related. We prefer to receive books for review in epub or mobi format. Feel free to send ebooks without querying first. We have reviewed about 14% of items received, though many of those reviewed are things we've actively requested from places like NetGalley.

Mission statement: The primary goal of *Theaker's Quarterly Fiction* is to keep going. If you're wondering why we do something a particular way, our primary goal is probably why.

Copyright and legal: All works are copyright the

Published in Theaker's Paperback Library on 4 July 2016.

Other Books

Theaker's Quarterly Fiction #9–54
Stephen Theaker and John Greenwood (eds)

Theaker's Quarterly Fiction #1–8
Stephen Theaker (ed.)

Space University Trent: Hyperparasite
Walt Brunston

There Are Now a Billion Flowers
The Hatchling (forthcoming)
John Greenwood

The Mercury Annual
Pilgrims at the White Horizon
Michael Wyndham Thomas

The Conan Doyle Weirdbook
Rafe McGregor (ed.)

Professor Challenger in Space
Quiet, the Tin Can Brains Are Hunting!
The Fear Man
Howard Phillips in His Nerves Extruded
Howard Phillips and The Doom That Came to Sea Base Delta
Howard Phillips and The Day the Moon Wept Blood
Stephen Theaker

Five Forgotten Stories
John Hall

Elephant
Harsh Grewal

Elsewhere
Steven Gilligan

New Words #1–4
John Greenwood, Steven Gilligan
and Stephen Theaker (eds)

Forthcoming Attractions

Thank you for a great issue, Howard!

Expect **Theaker's Quarterly Fiction #56** in August (then #57 in October and #58 in December).

We have enough submissions in hand for #56 and #57, so we are now only open to submissions for #58, the **Unsplatterpunk Special** edited by Douglas Ogurek, and that one is open to submissions until **August 31**. See below for Douglas's guidelines!

Reviews and additional instalments in ongoing serials are welcome at any time. We plan to open to regular submissions again in December for #59, due out March 2017.

Our blog is rather more active now:
www.theakersquarterly.blogspot.com

Stephen tweets every few days or so at:
www.twitter.com/Rolnikov

The zine now has its own Twitter account too, though we keep forgetting the password, so don't expect a quick reply: **www.twitter.com/TheakersQrtly**

Our email address is:
theakersquarterlyfiction@gmail.com

Call for Submissions: Unsplatterpunk Special!

Just a storyful of splatter makes the medicine go down.

If ever there were a subgenre that demonstrates the idiom, "Don't judge a book by its cover," unsplatterpunk is it. Unsplatterpunk offers the same vile ingredients of splatterpunk, literature's most extreme progeny, with one exception: somewhere within all that nastiness, unsplatterpunk offers a message that promotes virtue.

TQF is seeking fiction or satire submissions (no poetry please) for an unsplatterpunk special slated for publication in December of this year. Please note that TQF is a non-paying hobby zine, so if writing fiction is your job, this won't be the project for you; this is for the dilettantes, the hobbyists, the Saturday afternoon softball players and Sunday morning footballers. As always, the zine will be available free in PDF, epub and mobi formats, as well as on Kindle and in print via Amazon at the cheapest possible price.

TQF regular Douglas J. Ogurek will edit the issue. Here's Douglas:

Ever heard Sir Philip Sidney's dictum that literature should "teach and delight?" We're going to apply that sage advice to horror's most controversial subgenre: splatterpunk. Well, maybe "teach and disgust" is more appropriate in this case.

Unsplatterpunk has all the gore, depravity, and violence of splatterpunk, *plus* it embeds a positive message. Advice:

- Offend John and Jane Doe in the first couple of sentences
- Make story concept as attention-getting as a balloon popping at a party

- Approach your subject matter with a 14-year-old boy's mentality, but align your technique with that of a literary virtuoso
- Incorporate a positive message
- Try to avoid revenge or comeuppance stories: they often fail to teach a virtue

So give us your taboo and your controversial. Give us your cartoonish violence and over-the-top carnage. Just don't forget the positive message.

Deadline: 31 August 2016
Word count: 500–10,000
Reprints: No
Multiple submissions: No
Simultaneous submissions: No

File name:
Unsplatterpunk_[story title]_[author surname]

Payment: Non-paying zine (free epub, mobi and pdf copies available to everyone including contributors) plus recognition for helping create a new subgenre

Send submissions as a .doc or .rtf attachment, along with a 3rd person bio, to TQFunsplatterpunk@gmail.com. Please include UNSPLATTERPUNK in the subject line.